STARBOUND SOUL

BOOK FOUR OF THE GOBLIN STAR

By Gama Ray Martinez

God of Neverland *

Oracles of Kurnugi

Pharim War
Shadowguard
Veilspeaker
Beastwalker
Lightgiver
Darkmask
Lifebringer
Shadeslayer

Nylean Chronicles
Under the Moon
Child of the Wilde
Under the Sun
Child of the Stars

** Forthcoming*

STARBOUND SOUL

BOOK FOUR OF THE GOBLIN STAR

GAMA RAY MARTINEZ

Tolwis

CHAPTER 1

Radek hated the smell of mint. It wasn't mint exactly. Elven plants, the kind stuck in the ground, not the elves themselves, produced a chemical whose name Radek couldn't remember but that smelled almost exactly like mint. Since many of the cities on the elven homeworld of Droshala had been formed by mystically manipulating the growth of massive trees, it wasn't something he was likely to get away from.

He had lain on the branch near the top of a particularly tall tree for nearly two hours. Stars dotted the night sky. Sol was almost directly above him, but of course, Earth had never really been his home. Treya, the system Radek had grown up in, wasn't visible from Droshala at this time of year, but he still scanned the sky. It was only when the dim star appeared on the eastern horizon that Radek realized he had been waiting for it.

Vanel was actually two stars, and the binary system had once been the location of the elven space station of the same name. More than that, it had been Radek's home for nearly two years before the goblin attack that had led to its destruction. He had lived here ever since. He took a deep breath as he wiped away tears. He really hated the smell of mint.

The branch shook under heavy footsteps. Radek didn't need to look to see who it was. Only two people ever came to this spot who lacked the elven grace of silent movement. One was Radek himself. The other was his dwarven friend, Brenna.

He sat up, and she froze, but she moved forward once she saw that it was him. In the moonlight, he could just make out her clay-red skin. Her stout clothes were better suited for a miner than a diplomat, though it had been over a year since she had worked as one. She wore a forced smile and sat down next to him.

"What are you doing here?" he asked.

She nodded toward the horizon. "*Vanel* is rising."

Radek bit his lower lip and nodded. *Vanel* had been her home too. They sat quietly for a long time, staring at that dim point of light in the sky. Finally, Brenna broke the silence.

"They're looking for you."

Radek didn't take his eyes from the star. "I'm getting so tired of lessons."

Brenna snorted. "There was a time when you would have killed to be taught magic."

Radek sighed. "There was a time I thought I could do something with it."

"The goblins are still out there."

"And we need something more than a half-trained sorcerer who can't even manage a gust of wind."

"You didn't need a gust of wind to destroy the nova dragon or the ring ship."

"I got lucky."

"Everyone else got lucky. You saved the galaxy. Twice."

"And failed to save *Vanel.*"

Brenna let out a long breath. "Radek, I don't mean to be rude, but *Vanel* was one station." If Radek hadn't known her so well, he might have missed her voice cracking. "Even that wasn't so much a defeat as it was…a stalemate."

Radek sighed. "That doesn't really make me feel better." He looked down the trunk of the massive tree. Even a few years ago, scaling that would have seemed impossible, but so much time living among elves had taught him to climb in a way few humans ever learned. He could climb almost as fast as he could walk now. "What lesson is it?"

Brenna fingered the stone squares hanging from the leather strap around her neck. Radek could just barely feel a soft hum of power coming from within. If he was in physical contact, he'd be able to distinguish between the four, but from a distance, all he could say was that they pulsed with dwarven power. Brenna smiled.

"Rune magic."

CHAPTER 2

Radek increased the pressure on the clay, moving his fingernail across the red substance. He had to be extra careful. Dwarves had straight fingernails, allowing them to make precise lines when drawing runes. Radek hadn't yet reached the point where he could infuse a rune through tools, and the curvature of his nails made the lines particularly difficult. This rune was about as simple as they came, however. It would only store a tiny bit of magic to be used by some other rune. Any fledgling rune mage could carve the inscription in his sleep. Radek tried not to think about the fact that he had been failing at this for weeks.

He turned his nail at a slight angle. Blue light flashed from within the lines, and pain shot up his arm. Instinctively, Radek pulled back. The square of clay sizzled and turned black before flaking away to ash. Radek barely had time to brace himself before the switch slashed at his ear.

"How many times do I have to tell you?" the gruff rune mage said. "If you start to lose the crafting, seal it off. If there had been more than a speck of power in that clay, it would have burned off a finger."

Radek bit his lower lip and struggled to keep calm. "Yes, Master Gronun."

"And I told you to slow the flow of power. Even a botched rune shouldn't have had enough energy to do *that* to the clay."

"I'll try to do better next time, Master Gronun."

"I have never seen anyone with such raw power that is so lacking in skill."

Radek clenched his teeth. "I'm sorry, Master Gronun."

"That's enough for today. Practice crafting runes without using any power." He sniffed. "Assume you'll fail at half of them and practice the sealing. I don't want you blowing up my laboratory next time."

Radek stood up and bowed his head. "I'll do my best, Master Gronun."

"See that you do. I'm getting tired of the smell of burning clay."

Radek flushed but didn't say anything. Instead, he just bowed his head and slinked out of the room. As he did, the dwarven workshop's earthy scent faded, to be replaced by the verdant smells of the elven world. Ovian sat on a branch nearby.

"Master Inalin sent me to make sure you made it on time."

Radek tapped his wrist computer to bring up the time. "We still have half an hour."

"I know. I just…" He let out a breath. "I'm going to come with you."

Radek raised an eyebrow at that. "Ovian, you're already good at wind magic, probably better than I'll ever be."

Ovian looked upward. "You're catching on."

"That's not what I meant. Why would you come to a lesson where I'm probably going to try for two hours to make a gust strong enough to rustle a few leaves? You can already blow a man off his feet."

"It's just…I…"

Ovian sighed, and not for the first time, Radek realized how much his friend had wilted since the destruction of *Vanel*. At the end of the battle, the station had already been lost, and the goblins had been on the verge of stealing information that might well have won them the war. Even in hindsight, leaders and generals all agreed that destroying *Vanel* had been the only option, but Ovian was the one who had actually done it by transmitting the self-destruct command. He had never forgiven himself for that. Radek wished he could spend some time with him. Suddenly, an idea popped into his head.

"The fundamentals," he said. "You probably want to practice the fundamentals again. I bet that's a smart thing to do."

Ovian let out a breath and hopped off the branch onto the much larger one Radek stood on. "That's it. I want to make sure I haven't forgotten anything."

"It'll be nice for someone to be able to do something in that class."

As a shaper, the rarest of human mages, Radek had the ability to manipulate the magic of other races. He was still woefully inept at actually casting it, but his teachers all thought that by learning the principles of each race's magic, he would be better able to change what others had already cast. It made sense. Radek just wished he didn't have to spend hours each day feeling like an idiot.

Master Inalin's practice grounds were a dozen trees over, near the top. They took the full half-hour to get there, though either of them could have gotten there in a fraction of the time. Inalin was one of the only heavyset elves Radek had ever seen. That always seemed somehow wrong in a master of the air, but Inalin was widely regarded as the most skilled wind mage on Droshala.

"Ovian," Inalin said. "I'm surprised to see you here. I refused your request to join this lesson."

Radek glanced at his friend but didn't say anything. Instead, he turned to Inalin. The wind master, like all the master mages Radek had studied under, had always seemed so intimidating, so powerful. Inalin might well have reason for denying Ovian, but right now, Radek really didn't care. He knew it was regarded as a mark of status for an elven singer to be his trainer. He might as well get something out of it too.

"I'm not staying either."

"Ambassador Radek, your training…"

"Is voluntary. No one is forcing me to do it. For that matter, Ovian can probably teach me what I need to know about wind magic."

"He's hardly a trainer."

"I don't need to be able to use wind magic. I just need to know how it works."

Inalin raised a hand and opened his mouth. Then, he looked at Ovian before glancing toward the sky. "Oh, very well. He can stay. Let's start from where we left off, shall we?"

The master held one hand palm up, and a miniature whirlwind materialized. He raised an eyebrow at Radek, who clenched his jaw. He concentrated, trying to feel the wind, to make it a part of himself. He held out his hand and allowed his thoughts to flow. The power was there. He could feel it. He allowed it to take form and sang a single word before opening his eyes.

Nothing happened.

Radek let out a breath of frustration and tried again. The second time had no greater success than the first, and by the third, his head throbbed. Ovian had managed half a dozen whirlwinds in that time, all of them floating around his head.

Radek threw up his arms. "This is pointless."

"Nonsense," the elven master said. "You've seen all that your friend can do with wind magic."

"And even if I studied a thousand years, I'll never be as good as him. It's not like we're going to be calling blasts of air when we're fighting in *Wind*. Why don't I study something I'm actually going to use?"

"Like what?"

Radek hesitated, but only for a second. "Death magic."

No one said anything for several seconds. It was Ovian who finally broke the silence.

"Radek, you can't be serious. You can't learn necromancy."

"Why not?"

"Because you can't learn about the magic of the next world without learning about that world in the first place. You'd have to study it, and that…" he shuddered, though the air held the perpetual warmth of an elven spring. "It changes people."

"He is right," the elven master said. "It's the most dangerous field of magic there is. Even a master singer wouldn't teach necromancy to anyone who isn't at least two centuries old and who hasn't mastered two other fields of magic."

"Then, maybe I shouldn't learn from an elf."

Inalin stared at him, only blinking when Radek got up. The master called after him, but Radek ignored him. He gripped the trunk and began climbing down. A few seconds later, Ovian had joined him. In spite of the time Radek had spent here, he was still clumsy by comparison to even an elf like Ovian, who had spent most of his life in space. The elven boy easily kept pace with him.

"Where are we going?"

"I don't know. Anywhere. I'm just tired of wasting my time."

Half a dozen expressions flickered across the elf's face in a matter of seconds, but he didn't say anything. Finally, he stared into the forest. There was no way he could have seen through the thick woods, but Radek knew Ovian had guessed where he wanted to go.

"Let's go practice in *Wind*."

CHAPTER 3

Radek remembered when the sight of the *Stellar Wind* excited him. The sleek ship was quite possibly the most advanced in the galaxy. Built by a dragon, it had helped him, Ovian, and Brenna save the galaxy multiple times. And once, it hadn't been enough.

The docking bay was in a hollowed section of one of the great trees, and elven ships lined the chamber. Unlike human or dwarven shipyards, which always seemed to smell of rust and oil, elven magic gave the place the faint smell of flowers. *Wind* sat off to one side, elven and dwarven scientists scurrying around. Brenna spoke with a small cluster of them, but she looked up as they approached. A smile formed on her face, and she shouted orders. Some of the scientists grumbled but backed away. They had been studying the ship, and while they could only begin to understand how the dragon vessel functioned, every little piece they did discover had been used to further enhance the ships of the Compact.

"That was fast," Brenna said.

"What was fast?" Ovian asked.

She blinked. "You didn't get my message?"

Radek and Ovian exchanged glances before both shrugged.

Brenna let out a breath. "General Verren wants us to tour the fleet in *Wind*."

Ovian's brow furled. "Why?"

Brenna rolled her eyes. "Because most people haven't seen anything like her, and because the goblins are stronger than anyone thought. It will help a lot of people to see a dragon ship on our side."

"Contact Rania," Radek said. "She'll send a dragon ship."

Brenna scowled. "None of Rania's ships stopped the nova dragon or the ring ship."

Her eyes looked like they were made of steel, and after a few seconds, he threw his hands up and sighed. "Fine. I guess it doesn't make a difference. We were going to go flying anyway."

Brenna nodded once. Ovian met his eyes for a second before nodding. At a command from Radek, a hatch lowered under *Wind*. They got on and were lifted into the ship. A green dragon's face appeared on the viewscreen.

"Greetings, Radek, Ovian, Brenna."

"*Wind*," Radek said. "Can you detect the Compact fleet?"

The avatar inclined her head. "Thirty-seven capital ships are in orbit as well as numerous mid-sized vessels and fighters. Do you wish them enumerated?"

Radek waved that off. "We're going up for a demonstration. Will you inform General Verren that we're on our way?"

The screen flickered and was replaced with a map of space. Droshala floated like a green marble in the center. Around the Elven world, several dots indicating the various ships blinked. *Wind*'s voice sounded over the speakers.

"You may proceed when ready."

"Full speed into orbit."

"Through the atmosphere?" Brenna asked. "The friction will drain half of our shields."

"Twelve percent," *Wind* said.

Radek grinned. "It will give them quite a light show. *Wind* go."

Before anyone could say anything else, the ship shot up into the sky. Instantly, they were surrounded by a bubble of shimmering yellow energy. Wind's proximity sensors beeped as it approached the fleet. Suddenly, the bubble vanished. Radek caught a glimpse of flames licking the ship before the last remnant of atmosphere around the vessel burned away, revealing the Vanelian fleet.

The smooth elven vessels were the most prominent, but harsh angled dwarven ships nearly matched their numbers. A smattering of merfolk bubble ships and pointed human vessels could also be seen. Sensors detected the irregular shape of a were-creature capital ship, but it was so far Radek could barely make it out. It was one of the most impressive gatherings of warships Radek had ever seen. He just hoped it would be enough.

Wind beeped to indicate an incoming communication. At Radek's signal, the green dragon face faded to be replaced by a sharp-nosed elf with silver hair.

"Well, that was certainly impressive."

"General Verren," Brenna said. "You said you wanted to see us."

"Indeed, I did. With so much of the fleet here, I wanted to show them an example of our capabilities."

Ovian's face lit up, and he sat forward. "A war game?"

The general inclined his head. "Why don't you show us exactly what you can do?"

CHAPTER 4

Thirty-seven minutes. That was how long *Wind* lasted against the gathered ships before the simulated damage indicated destruction. Against two dozen capital ships, three times as many mid-sized vessels and nearly a hundred starfighters, they lasted thirty-seven minutes. In the process, they had managed to destroy or incapacitate nearly ten percent of the fleet and severely damage twice as many. Radek knew that it was only because the dragon-inspired enhancements to the Vanelian fleet that they hadn't done even more damage. *Wind* was advanced even by dragon standards.

Wind beeped, indicating an incoming communication, and the general's face appeared on the screen.

"Remarkable," Verren said. "Imagine if we had a whole fleet of those. Do you have any word on when more dragon ships will be delivered?"

Radek shrugged. "Soon, Rania said."

The elf chuckled. "Soon, according to a being who spent thousands of years living inside a sun. I have a feeling that decades could go by without her noticing."

Radek gave him a half-smile. "Maybe. How is work on your own artificial intelligence?"

The general shook his head. "Not well. The programming is too advanced. Even with your ship's help, we can't understand it. For now, *Stellar Wind* is the only one of its kind."

Brenna sighed and Radek gave the general a slow nod. A fleet of ships like *Wind* could have won the war in short order. For now, they would have to do it the slow way. At a command from Radek, *Wind* descended into the atmosphere, and they came down on the landing platform. *Wind* lowered them down, and as soon as Radek stepped out from under the ship, he froze. There, near the trunk of the great tree, stood an elderly human pair. The man was tall, nearly six feet, and had hair and eyes almost the exact color of steel. The woman was shorter and had a long nose and thin smile. Her pale blue eyes lit up when they saw him. The pair stepped forward, and for a moment, Radek didn't know what to do. It had been almost two years since he'd seen them, just after his father had been killed.

"Grandpa, grandma. What are you doing here?"

The old man laughed as he swept Radek up in an embrace. "What do you mean what are we doing here? We came to see you." He smiled. "Unless you've gotten too important to spend time with us. Now, why don't you introduce us to your friends?"

Radek looked over his shoulder. Brenna's face had lightened in embarrassment, but Ovian wore a wide grin. Radek felt his face heat up.

"These are Brenna, and you already met Ovian in the hospital on Treya. Brenna, Ovian, these are my grandparents, Rick and Mary Almon."

His grandfather bowed his head. "The heroes of the galaxy."

Brenna grew even lighter. "We didn't do that much."

"We did plenty," Ovian said. "You just weren't there for most of it."

"One time," Brenna said. "I wasn't there one time, and that was only because that happened before you knew me."

Ovian smirked. "Yeah, you're always making excuses."

"That's not an excuse! I was still a miner when you found the nova dragon."

Ovian nodded once. "Right. Like I said. Excuses."

Radek cleared his throat, and his companions looked at him. They both had the grace to look at least a little embarrassed. Radek waved at both his friends and his grandparents before walking to the trunk. He started to climb down but paused. He might be going an easy way as far as elves were concerned, but even that was beyond what he could have done a year ago. For his grandparents, climbing down the nearly smooth bark would be impossible. He gave them a questioning look. His grandfather nodded and held up a glowing green crystal. Ovian grinned.

"You got a light crystal!"

Radek raised an eyebrow. "It's day."

"No, not that kind of light crystal. The kind that makes you light."

"That's right," Radek's grandfather said. "It makes climbing a lot easier if you only weigh half as much as normal."

"Couldn't they have sent a transport?" Radek asked.

His grandfather shrugged. "I suppose they could have." He grinned. "But that wouldn't have been any fun. Now, where exactly are we going?"

Radek led them to the quarters he shared with Ovian. In spite of their age, Radek's grandparents moved through the trees gracefully, most likely the result of the light crystal and the gravity on Droshala being only eighty percent of the gravity on Treya.

Radek's quarters were messy, but neither of his grandparents said anything about that. His grandmother pushed aside a stack of papers and sat on a stool that had grown directly out of the floor. His grandfather just stood by the door.

"How are you, Radek?"

Radek tried to meet his gaze, but he could only manage it for a second before looking away.

"I'm fine."

"We thought you'd come back to Treya."

Radek shook his head. "There's a war. We have to fight it."

"Don't you think that sort of thing is better handled by someone a little older than thirteen?"

Radek looked away. "You mean if someone older had been in charge, *Vanel* wouldn't have been destroyed."

Ovian's jaw dropped. "Radek…"

Radek's grandpa had already raised a hand. Ovian inclined his head.

"Now, that's not fair," his grandpa said. "You've done as much as anyone could expect, and more than most. I just think what you've taken on is too heavy a burden for you."

"I'll be fine."

"I've no doubt of that. You're too strong for anything else. Your father was the same way, but he never—"

"The goblins killed him!" Radek cried out. "They killed him, Ovian's father, leveled entire merfolk cities, and destroyed *Vanel.*" Even now, his voice choked on the name of the space station. "I can't just leave the war and go back to Treya. There's too much to do."

"Let someone else handle it," his grandmother said, "at least for a little while. You don't have to come back to Treya. Just find some place away from the war to rest for a few days."

"I can't," Radek said. "I'm the ambassador to the dragons."

"Radek," Brenna said, "as far as we know, there's not a big battle coming up. Maybe they're right. You could take a break." She looked toward Ovian. "We all could. It's not like they wouldn't tell us if something happened."

"She's right," Ovian said, "they'd never want to go into battle without *Wind.*"

Radek bit his lower lip and thought for a second before shaking his head. "There's no time. I can't let there be another *Vanel.*"

Ovian spoke softly. "It's not like you pushed the button that destroyed it."

"You had to," Radek said. "You know your father would have done it if he'd been able to."

"What about the other thousands of people on *Vanel?* Would they have done it? My father ordered me, but I made the choice for so many others."

"No," Radek said, "It wasn't about that. You had to, or the goblins could have gotten *Wind*'s full schematics. If they built another ring ship, they could have a fleet of *Wind*s. Rania gave her to us. You couldn't let the goblins learn how to build another."

Ovian looked like he was going to argue, but instead, he bowed his head once. Unshed tears welled in his eyes. He opened his mouth to speak and closed it again after a few seconds, all words having fled from him.

They stayed that way for a long time. Radek never said what he'd been thinking. It hadn't been Ovian's fault. By the time Ovian had given the order that destroyed *Vanel,* there had been no choice. If Radek had been able to help in the battle with the evil wizard Derek, if he had been able to stop the goblins from taking over the water elementals, if he had been able to do *something* in the battle for *Vanel* other than rely on *Wind*…

It was all Radek's fault.

CHAPTER 5

Radek rolled the control sphere, and *Wind* veered to one side. The goblin bean weapon bounced off the shield.

"Too close," he said under his breath. "*Wind*, reduce the shield radius to fifty percent."

"At that range, the expulsion of energy from a breach could cause significant damage."

"Do it anyway. We're losing too much energy to these glancing shots. That one should have missed us entirely."

The ship's avatar bowed her head, and the shield indicator screen showed their defenses shrinking to half their original size. Radek shouted a command, and the blue beam shot forth, impacting the carrier ship. Ice crystals spewed out of the hull breach as the water elemental was pulled into the cold of space.

Another blast, this one, from a Necal capital ship, engulfed *Wind*. Radek maneuvered the ship out of the danger zone just as a communication notification appeared on his console. He dismissed it and fired a stellar core missile at the rebel dwarves. He didn't bother to see the result. Runestone ships were incredibly resilient, and even a stellar core missile wasn't enough to destroy them entirely, but it would be enough damage to take them out of the fight. With this many enemies around Radek, that would have to be good enough.

Wind rocked as a beam of light engulfed them. The strength of the blast lit up the shields into an opaque shell. Alarms blared. Radek tried to maneuver out of the beam, but the controls responded sluggishly.

The shields went out. The energy of that alone would have severely damaged the starfighter, but they were still in the midst of the beam weapon. The hull screeched as pieces were torn off. *Wind*'s alarms blared once more before everything went black.

After a few seconds, the black peeled back, revealing the docking bay's wooden interior that had been grown inside the great tree. *Wind*'s status displays showed the results of the simulation. The starfighter, of course, had never actually taken off. Holograms projected onto the cockpit had given the illusion of reality, while short bursts from thrusters had helped to simulate damage. Radek's more aggressive tactics had led to them being destroyed a few minutes into the Battle of *Vanel* rather than surviving to the end of it. He had replayed the battle over and over again, trying nearly two dozen strategies. All ended the same way. Failure.

"What were you doing?" Ovian's voice said.

Radek blinked and looked around. It took him a second to realize that his friend's voice had come out of the ship's speakers. The elf stood at the entrance to the docking bay, wearing a half-grin. Radek sighed and got up. *Wind* lowered him to the ground. By the time he stepped on solid bark, Ovian had come near. The elf raised an eyebrow.

"Well?"

For a second, Radek considered making something up, but one look at his friend's face told him it wouldn't do any good.

"You already know, don't you?"

Ovian bit his lower lip and nodded. "I had *Wind* project whatever you were seeing onto the ceiling." He hesitated before letting out a breath. "How long were you doing that?"

Radek shrugged. "Just a few minutes. I only did one simulation."

Ovian gave him a hard look. "Radek, I watched the last three."

"Why didn't you say anything?"

"Why didn't you stop?"

"Because…" Radek took a couple of deep breaths. "Because there has to be something else we could have done."

"Even if there was, what good would it do now?"

"I don't know!" Radek cried out. "I just have to do something. I can't just keep sitting here feeling sorry for myself."

"Radek, we're helping to run a war. There's a lot to do. You don't have to keep reliving this." There were tears in the elf's eyes. "How can you stand it?"

Radek stammered for a second. "I'm sorry. You shouldn't have had to see that. It's not your fault *Vanel* was destroyed."

Ovian breathed deeply. "It's not your fault either."

Radek looked back at *Wind* and closed his eyes. He reached up to wipe at his face, and his fingers came back wet. He scanned the docking bay. Though he knew some of the elven vessels had taken part in the battle six months before, they no longer showed any damage. In fact, because of *Wind*'s enhancements, they were even more capable than they had been.

"I'm not sure. Maybe if…"

"No," Ovian said. "There's no maybe. If it wasn't my fault, then it definitely wasn't yours."

They stood in silence for what felt like an hour before Radek said something. "Is that why you came? To see what I was doing?"

Ovian blinked and shook his head. "No. Sorry. Brenna tried to send you a communication a couple of times, but you didn't answer."

Radek shrugged. "I was busy."

Ovian glanced at *Wind* before looking up at the ceiling. "Right. Well, anyway, Brenna wants us to go to dinner at the dwarven enclave tonight."

Radek rolled his eyes. "I'm getting tired of all these state dinners and official functions. If we spent half as much time getting ready for the war as we do practicing politics, we would have beat the goblins already."

Ovian smirked. "Actually, Silver Balena's shuttle just landed. She wanted to give us an update on the positioning of the Runestone Fleet."

Radek perked up. Balena was one of the highest-ranking members of the dwarven military, responsible for the deployment of their fleet and overseer of military action in a dozen key systems. She also happened to be Brenna's mother.

"I mean, if you're busy," Ovian said in an exaggerated tone, "I can tell her that we'll meet with her some other time. I hear she just got back from goblin space, but I'm sure she'll understand."

Radek glared at him. "You're not funny."

Ovian let out a bark of laughter. "So, are you coming?"

CHAPTER 6

Dinner consisted of a variety of different kinds of fruit. Like most elven food, it was sweet, and the smell of mint filled the air. Balena eyed them as they took their first bite. Ovian smiled, and the dwarven general chuckled.

"A bit better than last time, wouldn't you say?"

Ovian laughed. "You mean when you forced us to eat that greasy mess?"

Even Radek found himself grinning. The last time Balena had hosted them, she had been the newly assigned dwarven ambassador to *Vanel*. They had been served dwarven food, and Ovian had been vocal about his disapproval of that.

Brenna laughed. "We hardly forced you to eat it, and besides, braised salamander is a delicacy."

Some of the color drained from Ovian's face? "I ate lizard?"

Brenna laughed. "It was a year ago, Ovian. If you haven't gotten sick by now, I'm pretty sure you're not going to."

Ovian groaned and laid his head on the table. "I'm not so sure."

"What did you learn from goblin space?" Radek asked.

Slowly, the laughter subsided, and everyone looked at him. Balena popped a piece of blue fruit into her mouth. She winced at the sour flavor of the bern berry but swallowed it anyway.

"Right to business, I see. Very well. I took a dozen stealth capable ships. We scattered to gather intelligence, but only three of us made it back to the rendezvous." She sighed. "It's not good news. The goblins are stronger than expected. The Necal have been helping in their shipbuilding efforts, but even that doesn't account for what we saw. They seem to have enhancements to shields, weapons, stealth systems, scanners, and about half a dozen other areas of technology. I can't be sure, but I think they've had help."

Radek didn't want to say it, but the words came out almost of their own accord. "Dragon technology."

Brenna's face darkened, but her mother nodded as she waved her hand over the table. A spot in the middle of the wood glowed blue, and dwarven numbers appeared in the air over the table. It took Radek a second to mentally translate them, as Balena explained.

"That would be my guess. If not for what we learned from studying your ship's blueprints, I doubt any of us would have made it back. There's more. Counting only what the ships that survived saw, the goblins have more ships than they should."

Ovian groaned. "You think they have another ring ship."

The dwarf inclined her head. "Either that or the goblins discovered some other way to quickly build a fleet of starships."

"Then, we have to strike quickly," Radek said.

Balena sighed. "If only it were that easy. In my estimation, they already have enough ships to fortify their space."

"But if we keep waiting, they'll just build more," Radek pointed out.

"And then, they'll overrun us." Brenna said.

"What are we going to do?" Ovian asked.

"In that regard, I do have an idea," Balena said. "A way we might be able to bypass all the goblin defenses and hit Goalton directly."

Radek leaned forward. Travel through hyperspace didn't go through the physical world, but it could still be detected, especially around a homeworld. No doubt half the goblin fleet could be recalled to defend the goblin homeworld the moment a force of any size was detected, effectively making a surprise attack impossible. Silver Balena taking a handful of ships was one thing, but that was completely different from a fleet large enough to assault an entire planet. On the other hand, Brenna's mother was hardly a fool.

"How?" Radek asked.

The dwarven woman smiled. "You recall how swiftly you got from Avuana to *Vanel?*"

Radek stiffened. "Yes, but that took a lot of magic. We basically had to steal it from warring merfolk gods." He looked to Ovian. "Are there any elven gods that could help us?"

Ovian huffed. "We stopped believing in those centuries ago."

Radek shrugged. "That was before we met two of them."

"Will you two stop that?" Brenna asked. "Mother, they do have a point. Where do you propose we get that much magic?"

"The elves."

"We don't have that much," Ovian said. "I mean, we might be able to transport one or two ships, maybe, but even that would have to be starfighters, not capital ships."

"Actually, I think you do." She grinned and held out a data crystal. "I've received intelligence reports that one of your spies has just recovered a valuable crystal."

The circle in the middle of the table hummed, and a hologram of a round gem appeared in the air. Balena tapped one of the facets, and the image zoomed in, transforming into a variety of interconnecting lines. Radek had studied elven magic enough to know that this was a crystal matrix, but he didn't know enough to actually understand what it meant. Ovian, on the other hand, gasped and raised his hand toward the illusion.

"It can't be."

"What?" Radek asked.

"That was lost on Earth millennia ago."

"What was?"

"We all assumed it had been destroyed."

Radek glared at his friend. "Ovian, if you don't tell me what you're talking about, I'm going to hit you."

Ovian blinked and looked at him. "Oh, sorry. Do you remember that time we found a perfect ruby in Rania's lair?"

Radek nodded. "You said it could hold a lot of enchantments."

"Well, this one is even *more* perfect."

"Something can't be more perfect," Brenna said. "That's kind of the point of being perfect."

Ovian looked at the ceiling. "You just don't understand how magic works." He let out a long breath and shook his head. "It's too complicated to explain. That diamond, assuming it is what I think it is…" He looked to Balena, who nodded, "held an elven curse for thousands of years after we left Earth. I don't think the humans ever realized what it was."

"Wait," Radek said. "*After* you left Earth? You mean this was from…before?"

Ovian nodded. "When all the races still lived on Earth. It was cursed then, and it held the curse nearly perfectly. If we empowered that…" He stared at the matrix for several seconds. "We could do almost anything."

"It was on Earth?" Brenna asked.

Ovian nodded without looking away. "I had heard that it was lost in the last great human war before they rediscovered their magic."

Radek swallowed. "Burning Sky."

As soon as he said it, he realized what he was looking at. The War of the Burning Sky had been what humans had feared since they first learned to split the atom, a nuclear war. It hadn't lasted long, but it had devastated the entire planet, and destroyed most major cities, including the city that had once held this treasure. Radek's mouth went dry.

"You mean the Hope Diamond really was an elven crystal?"

Ovian nodded as a smile crept onto his face. "And now, we can use it to end this war."

CHAPTER 7

Radek gaped at the tall elven figure that stood before the leaders of the Vanelian Compact. They sat in a round room with a raised platform. The elf, whom Verren had identified as Yevul, stood in the center as he recounted the story of recovering the gem from a group of possessed shape changers.

"Wererats?" General Verren said, turning to Ableran, the wereboar head of the shapeshifter delegation. "Didn't your people think that it might be wise to deliver such a powerful weapon into the hands of those who could best use it?"

The wereboar snorted. "I doubt very much they knew they had an elven crystal, and they certainly never suspected its curse would destroy them." He waved off the accusation. "We can't be held responsible for what every rogue band of pirates does."

"Enough with the politicking," Silver Balena said. "The important thing is we have it now." She turned to Verren. "Well? Can it do what I think?"

"I still think a weapon would be a better choice."

"What do you call the ability to nearly instantly move an entire fleet behind enemy lines? We could end the war tomorrow."

Ambassador Brenton, the ambassador from Earth, shook his head. "Even if we could figure out how to duplicate Radek's feat, I doubt it would be quick." He glanced at General Verren, who nodded. "We won't be able to move soon, and the question is if we can keep this information from the enemy. If they get even a hint of what we're capable of, they'll retreat back to Goalton. If that happens, we can forget about ending this war quickly."

"I can hide the information," the elf in the center of the room said.

Verren shivered at his voice but nodded. "Yevul is one of our best operatives. If anyone can keep this hidden, he can."

"But can he duplicate the spell?"

Yevul turned his cold blue eyes to Radek, and a chill crawled down his spine. He could have sworn the temperature in the room dropped several degrees. "I assume I'll have him available to help."

"Radek may be accomplished, but he's only a child," Brenton said.

Radek hadn't been looking forward to working with the dark elf, but the human ambassador's words made his face heat up in anger. He stood up to speak, but the elven spy waved him off. Yevul just snorted at Brenton. "How old are you? I'm no good at guessing human ages, but I'd say, fifty?"

Brenton stiffened. "I don't see what that has to do with anything."

"Then, consider this. On this last assignment, I reached my fourth century of life. I understand the boy is thirteen. That would make him only thirty-seven years younger than you." The elf chuckled. "I don't think you can comprehend how little four decades means to me. You and he are equally children."

"Well, that may be, but…"

"And from what I hear, he is one of the ambassadors to the dragons, so his rank is equal to, if not greater than yours. He may be of your race, but he is not under your command." Brenton's face was red with fury, but if Yevul noticed, he gave no sign. Instead, he turned back to Radek, giving him that same bone-chilling gaze. "What do you say, boy? Will you help me craft this enchantment?"

Radek swallowed and looked to Ovian. The elf was staring at Yevul with wide-eyed awe. It was only when Radek cleared his throat that Ovian blinked and nodded. He wished Brenna were here, but this meeting had only been for diplomats, and only Radek and Ovian had been selected by Rania. Finally, Radek nodded.

"I'll help."

The dark elf inclined his head. "Good. Now, why don't we get started right away?"

CHAPTER 8

It was frustratingly difficult to empower the gem to do what they wanted. On Avuana, the gods Tiamat and Bahamut had been releasing so much power that even a tiny fraction, guided by *Wind*'s own magic, had been enough to send them hurtling through hyperspace. It had been quick and dirty magic, but placing a persistent enchantment on an elven gem required methodically weaving the framework of the spell into the gem. To make matters worse, hyperspace travel was one of the most complicated weaves of any race. While Radek had experience with dragon magic, and to a lesser degree, goblin and dwarven magic, Ovian had always been the one to handle elven magic, and it was elven magic that had to be used to empower the crystal.

Yevul shook his head. "No, no, no. You're not holding the spell in place."

"I held it for twenty minutes," Radek said.

"And if you wanted to transport an insect twenty feet, that would be enough." The elf shook his head. "I told you, Radek, this is going to take hours. If you can't do that, tell me now, and we'll find some other way to use this crystal." For a moment, the elf allowed his gaze to settle on the Hope Diamond, which stood on a pedestal in a small room. Amber beads embedded in the ceiling provided a soft golden light that made the diamond almost shine. Yevul let out a breath. "I can think of a dozen ways that would be better than using it as a glorified troop transport."

Ovian glared at him. In elven society, rank was passed down, though it was possible to gain rank beyond your family's by distinguishing yourself. Ovian had been the son of the leader of the space station *Vanel,* and beyond that, their adventures together had given the elven boy a certain status of his own among his people. Radek didn't understand exactly how such things worked, but he was sure of one thing. Ovian far outranked an elven spy who, as far as he could understand, had no rank at all. Yevul should have been bowing before Ovian at the very least. Instead, he just pretended not to see him. Ovian ground his teeth.

"It's not just a troop transport," Ovian said. "We're taking capital ships and midsized cruisers. With a little luck, we'll end the goblins before they even know we're there."

Yevul shook his head. "It doesn't matter how effective it would be, not if we can't get it to work in the first place. Radek, try again."

Radek's head was pounding from all the effort, but he nodded and closed his eyes as Yevul called the magic again. Elven power poured into the crystals as Radek tried to hold the shape of the spell. Yevul's power felt like liquid fire as it touched Radek's own magic. He clenched his teeth. He was about to lose it. A drop of power slipped through his fingers. He couldn't hold on, but in the instant before he lost the spell entirely, heat suffused him. He had been so caught up in shaping the elven power that it took him a second to recognize what he was feeling.

"Dragon magic."

Yevul blinked. "What?"

"I feel dragon magic." Radek tapped his wrist communicator.

After a few seconds, Brenna's face appeared, and she wore a wide smile. "Radek, you won't believe it."

"Rania?" Radek guessed.

For a second, Brenna's eyes widened. She nodded. "More than that, she's brought a fleet of ships with her. We'll be able to use them when we attack the goblins!"

CHAPTER 9

For the past two years, *Wind* had been the most advanced ship anyone had ever seen. Now, the skies of Droshala were filled with sleek vessels that shimmered green in the light of the elven sun. Hope filled the air so thickly that Radek could almost see it. Still, he couldn't help but feel that they had lost something, now that their uniqueness was gone. He realized he was being childish, of course. This could be exactly what they needed. Sensors reported at least three dozen vessels, the stealth technology in these ships making a positive lock extremely difficult. Rania's transmission said she had brought twice that many.

"We can win." Brenna's voice cracked as she spoke. "With all these, we can actually win."

Balena nodded. The dwarven ambassador hadn't stopped smiling since she had heard the news. "If we can transport all of these behind the goblin lines, it won't even be a fight." She turned to Radek. "How close are we to doing that?"

"Not very." Radek spoke in a quiet voice, but then, he saw a red figure descending from the sky. His cheeks started aching from having so wide a smile. "But now, we have help."

The dragon came right at them, her wings casting a shadow over the wooden platform that the leaders of the compact had gathered on. Then, Rania's form shimmered as if being seen through waves of heat. Rania dove, and everyone around Radek, save Ovian and Brenna, scattered. At the last minute, Rania pulled up, as if to land. Her form seemed to melt away, and a woman with pale skin and emerald hair stepped onto the ground. The branch shuddered, though Radek had the sense it was more in response to the weight of her power than her physical body. Brenna gasped, and Ovian uttered something in Elven that Radek couldn't quite catch. Radek found himself staring.

"I...I didn't know you could do that."

The woman raised her eyebrow. "Of course. It's a rather simple transformation. Any dragon who bothered to learn would be able to do it. Few do, though."

"That's what I told him," Ovian said.

"No, you didn't."

Ovian made an exaggerated motion of rolling his eyes. Brenna chuckled.

"What was it you said, Ovian?" the dwarf asked. "By the eternal green?"

"Well," Ovian stammered. "I mean, I guess I did say that, but it's just an expression. I mean, my mother..."

He went silent, and it took Radek a second to understand. Malen, Ovian's mother, had orange eyes. Elven legend said that meant she had dragon blood in ancestry, which could obviously only happen if dragons could transform, as Rania had done. Ovian's mother, however, had been aboard *Vanel* when the goblins attacked.

Radek cleared his throat, trying to draw attention away from his grieving friend. "Is that why you came, Lady Rania? To deliver ships?"

"That, and more." She looked around. Some of the elves were already creeping closer. All had their eyes on Rania's humanoid form. "I am here to help. I understand you've had an idea."

"You did it once," Radek said after he had explained Balena's idea of moving the fleet. "So did we, when we flew from Avuana."

Rania nodded and motioned for them to follow. She walked to the edge of the wooden platform and leaped off, Radek ran to the edge and looked down. Once again in dragon form, Rania flew between the trees, heading for the docking bay that held *Wind.* The elves didn't need to be told. They scurried down the tree holding the platform and began jumping from branch to branch. Ovian started to climb down but stopped and looked at Radek and Brenna.

"Go ahead," Radek said. "We'll meet you there."

He nodded and took off after the others. Like Radek, Brenna had grown more skilled and moving through the trees in her time on the elven homeworld, but neither of them could match an elf who really wanted to move fast. Ovian leaped from branch to branch as if he were prancing on solid ground. Radek knew if he tried that, he'd become nothing more than a splat on the forest floor.

Radek and Brenna went as quickly as they could, even to the point of risking jumps they would normally have avoided. By the time they got to the docking bay, Radek's muscles ached, and Brenna's palm was bleeding from grabbing a branch that had been just a little too rough.

They walked into the docking bay gasping. He could see the resentment on the faces of the elves, but Rania, once again in human form, didn't give them a chance to say anything. She walked over to *Wind* and laid a hand on the hull. She grunted something that should not have been able to come from a humanoid throat. The window in front of the cockpit took on a blue glow. The image of a dragon, identical to Rania except for being green, appeared on the window. Radek and Ovian exchanged glances.

"Did you know she could do that?" Radek asked.

Brenna snorted. "How could you not know she could do that?"

Radek blinked. "You did?"

"You knew she could project holograms inside the cockpit, right?"

"Well, yes."

"And you realize that window is made of glass, right?"

Radek groaned. It made sense. If *Wind* could project images on one side of the window, then of course, she could do that to the other side. In fact, that was probably how Ovian had first noticed Radek's simulations.

Rania's eyes looked from one to the other, patiently waiting for their conversation to finish. When it appeared it was done, she spoke to the dragon image in Elven.

"*Stellar Wind*, show me the spell form for how Radek transported you."

The green dragon image inclined her head, and her form fuzzed. Lines appeared on the window, twisting into impossible shapes. They twisted and writhed so that Radek's eyes hurt to look at them. He turned away, but Ovian stared at the image with pure awe in his gaze. Some of the other gathered elves whispered to each other. After a few seconds, they all looked to Radek.

"You did that?" Ovian asked

Radek blinked. "Did what?"

"You used that to carry us through hyperspace? How did you not crush us?"

"The matrix to safely travel through hyperspace is embedded into my gold drive," *Wind* said. "Radek simply appropriated it and integrated it into his own spell."

Rania closed her eyes for a second. "Interesting. It would appear Radek's interactions with the ship's magic affected the artificial intelligence as well."

"Is *Wind* okay?" Radek asked.

"Yes, though it is somewhat more developed than before. You certainly left your mark. As to the spell, however—"

The lines shifted, expanding and contracting at seemingly random times. The elves all stared at it for several seconds without saying anything. The awe in their faces made Radek uncomfortable. Finally, Ovian spoke in a voice barely above a whisper.

"You were going to do that to an elven crystal?"

"I do not believe it would have worked," Rania said. "You were attempting to duplicate dragon magic using elven power and shaped with human magic before placing it inside of a container." She shook her head. "Such a thing is not impossible, though I suspect you are decades away from being able to achieve that feat. You are correct in thinking that it is similar to the spell I laid on the Vanelian system, though it is at the same time more simple and more complex."

"You understand it?" Ovian asked.

The dragon nodded. "I understand it, and with a little effort, I can duplicate it."

CHAPTER 10

Radek lay in bed, reflecting on the day. Elves, dwarves, and humans scrambled throughout the trees. Everyone who had ever flown a starfighter clamored for the opportunity to get one of the dragon vessels. Even some merfolk wanted the opportunity, though Rania hadn't designed the ships for their physiology. Silver Balena had asked Brenna, Radek, and Ovian for their opinion on the matter, but though the trio were almost universally highly regarded by the military, most of their missions had been on their own. They had trained, and *Wind* had records of their mock battles, but beyond that, the three of them weren't much use, so once again, they had been left to their own devices while the others prepared for the upcoming attack.

He sighed and rolled out of bed. He tapped the viewscreen on his wall to get a status update on the fleet. Everything was as expected. He was about to go back to bed when the orbital sensors detected a disturbance. An instant later, the alarms blared, and the viewscreen showed goblins coming into the system. Without bothering to change out of his pajamas, he ran out of his room.

The corridors of the tree base were awash with activity. Elven, dwarven, and human soldiers scrambled through the halls, trying to get to their ships. He even passed a merfolk tank as he ran. By the time Radek reached *Wind*, Ovian and Brenna were already there. Radek got into his seat, and *Wind* shot out of the docking bay before making an almost ninety-degree turn, zipping toward space.

"Status?" Radek asked.

"All systems are fully operational," *Wind* said.

"And the goblins?"

"Four carriers came out of hyperspace one light second away from Droshala. Each released a squadron."

"Four squadrons?" Brenna asked. "Forty-eight ships?"

"Plus the carriers," Ovian said. "They'll be as heavily armed as any elven ship."

The blue sky of the elven homeworld peeled away to reveal a starry sky. Part of the elven fleet had already engaged, and no one noticed *Wind* coming out of the atmosphere. Almost directly ahead of them sat one of the carriers, a box-like vessel brimming with weapons. Ovian hit a button, and a blue beam shot forward. The shield around the goblin carrier shimmered for a second before the plasma broke through it and pierced the ship. A heartbeat later, it exploded, taking a pair of fighters with it.

"That's three down," Brenna said as she examined one of the displays. "Thirty-eight left. We've been noticed."

Before either Radek or Ovian could reply, a missile crashed into *Wind*'s shield. The vessel rocked for a second before stabilizing. A quick scan of the status displays revealed there had been no damage. Radek and Ovian exchanged glances and smiled as Radek spun the control sphere. *Wind* turned sharply and fired a series of green energy balls. They splashed against a pair of goblins starfighters that were a little too close together. They shook, but their shields held.

"Well, that's new," Ovian said. "They've been upgraded."

"Focus the fire on just one."

Ovian nodded, but he was already making a change to the targeting system. He fired again, and this time, all the balls hit only one of the goblin ships. The shields went bright, but before they could break through, three of the goblin fighters focused their fire on *Wind*, and Radek had to move them away to avoid damage.

"Keep with the beam," Brenna said.

Ovian nodded but didn't say anything else. He fired the plasma beam canon again. This time, they broke through, and the goblin fighter exploded. *Wind*'s sensors beeped, and Radek realized a dozen goblin fighters were converging on their position.

"We won't be able to hold that many off," Brenna said. "Shield strength is already down."

"What about the rest of the fleet?"

"Approximately one-tenth of the fleet was in orbit when the attack took place," *Wind* said. "We were faster to mobilize than the rest. Estimate the remaining ships will engage the goblins in ninety seconds."

"I don't think we have ninety seconds." One of the dots on the proximity scanner disappeared, and Radek gaped for a second. "What was that?"

The scanner fuzzed, and when it cleared, it had focused in on a smaller area. A stream of letters across the screen told him it had switched to biological sensors, which had a shorter range. The dot moved toward another ship, and after a second, that fighter vanished as well. Radek felt a grin split his face. "Is that what I think it is?"

Wind's avatar appeared on the screen and inclined its head. "It is a dragon."

Radek, Ovian, and Brenna all spoke at the same time.

"Rania."

Radek almost laughed as Rania destroyed two more goblin ships. The remaining enemy vessels turned to attack the dragon, but by then, the rest of the elven fleet had made it to the battle. Elven ships had always been faster and more maneuverable than their goblin counterparts. That combined with advanced sensors and stealth technology meant that elven ships were, in general, far superior to those built by the goblins. A squadron of elven starfighters fired on half a dozen goblin ships in a maneuver that should have reduced them to dust, but a shimmering bubble of red energy appeared around the enemy vessels, holding off the blasts.

Radek and Ovian exchanged glances. Radek tapped one of the viewscreens, though he was already sure what he would see. That didn't stop him from gasping, though. The shields had a frequency unlike anything he had seen in ships built by the goblins, or the Necal, for that matter. The only place he had seen shields like that was around ancient dragon ships.

Radek pushed the control sphere forward, and *Wind* shot toward the enemy. Ovian tapped a button, and a missile streaked forward. *Wind* had been built by Rania herself, and for all her prowess in battle, Rania was, first and foremost, a scientist. She had spent centuries developing their ship. The goblin ships might have been augmented by dragon technology, but *Wind* was advanced even by the standard of dragons. The stellar core missiles slammed into the closest ship. The shield appeared but almost immediately winked out of existence. The three nearest goblin ships were also caught in the blast. They weren't destroyed, but they were damaged enough that the elven vessels mopped them up in short order.

The elves adjusted quickly to their enemy's unexpected toughness, changing their tactics so that they attacked only when they outnumbered their foes. Dwarven and human ships joined the battle, along with a handful of merfolk bubble ships. The fleet, combined with Rania, was too much for the goblins, and those few that weren't destroyed fled into hyperspace. A combined force of dwarves and elves disappeared after them. Radek almost did as well, but Rania's face appeared on the viewscreen. She spoke swiftly, sounding nervous in a way Radek hadn't realized dragons could.

"Radek, meet me near the main command building on the surface. I must speak with you and the leaders of this alliance."

"What is it?" Brenna asked. "Is everything okay?"

"Those vessels were altered using technology that they should not have had."

"I know," Radek said. "I saw that. We know they have dragon allies."

"Yes, I am aware, but that's not my point. Their weapons were based on principles of physics that other dragons don't know about. I discovered those myself, long after I withdrew from the rest of my people. Someone has access to my research."

"Oh no." Brenna's voice was barely above a whisper. "If they've really figured out how to duplicate *Wind*'s technology, then this is even worse than we thought. If they have another ring ship..."

Radek's blood felt like it turned to ice. "We could be facing a fleet of *Wind*s."

CHAPTER 11

The silver-haired elf stared up at Radek and his friends as they stood on the raised platform in the meeting room. "How could this happen?"

"We knew they had access to some of the information on *Stellar Wind*," Brenna said. "They used it to hijack us a year ago."

"That flaw was corrected," Silver Balena said.

Brenna inclined her head. "Still, to do it in the first place, they must have had access to at least some of the dragon vessel's schematics."

"We always thought there could be a spy," Radek said. "We saw a couple of signs after that, but nothing major, and we began to wonder if their dragon had done it on his own."

"Another dragon might have been able to take control of *Stellar Wind*'s programming," Rania, once again in humanoid form, said. "It is, however, doubtful that they would have been able to do so that quickly without access to at least some of the vessel's schematics. That was never one of Grr'ink'itor's skills, though."

"Grr'ink'itor?" the shapeshifter representative asked, doing an admirable job of duplicating Rania's pronunciation.

"The dragon that lives in the goblins' sun," Radek supplied.

"And you're sure this dragon couldn't have been the one to take over your ship's systems?"

Rania met the werebear's gaze, and he blanched and shuffled back a few steps. The faint hint of a smile appeared on Rania's face, though she suppressed it quickly. She bowed her head. "It is possible we are wrong, but I do not believe so. It is true that any security system can be defeated, but as I understand the circumstances, the goblins had intended to capture *Stellar Wind* in order to learn its secrets, so it stands to reason that they did not possess full schematics. Defeating a ship's security is completely different from duplicating its technology. Those advancements were developed by me, and the only way they could have gotten them is by stealing them."

"There's something else we're not considering," the human ambassador said. "Why did they attack in the first place. A raid that small wasn't enough to do significant damage. I'm sure they didn't come to just show off their new technology."

"No, but most likely to test it," Rania said. "I suspect there was a scout nearby watching."

"Regardless, what are we going to do about it?" General Verren asked. "If the goblins gain advanced technology in addition to the superior numbers a ring ship would provide, we may not be able to stop them."

Balena huffed. "Some of us don't surrender so easily."

The werebear growled in agreement, but General Verren scowled. "I am not suggesting we do, but we do have to do something, and we have to do it soon."

The dwarven ambassador grinned. "Haste from an elf?"

Verren gave her a level look. "If you are done mocking me, perhaps we can go onto planning? How is the spell progressing?"

Sound came from a shadow cast by the general. Radek jumped and stared into it. It was only then that he saw Yevul standing there. He wondered how long the elf had been there, but Yevul glided on the platform on silent steps. Some of the ambassadors backed up as he moved his gaze from one to another.

"We are nearly ready." He bowed to Rania. "With Lady Rania's help, the spell form is already in place. It will take a great deal of power, however. It will take three days for the singers to charge it. Then, we can perform a test. Three days later, assuming everything goes well, we will be ready to launch."

"Six days," General Verren said. "If there really is a spy, in six days, the goblins could know all our plans before we launch. This could all be for nothing if they're ready for us." He looked at the ceiling and sighed. "It's too long."

"Unless you want to assign more singers, that's the best we can do."

Verren exchanged glances with Inali, an elf who looked more like a gnarled tree than anything else. The old elf inclined his head. "How many singers?"

Yevul blinked. After a second's hesitation, he smirked. "If you give me the hundred most powerful singers on the planet, I could have it charged for testing in a few hours. Otherwise—"

"Fine," Inali said.

Yevul stared at him. "What?"

Inali was typing into his viewscreen. Radek saw half a dozen elven faces. He looked up. "They'll be here by the end of the day. I want the fleet to leave tomorrow. Can you do that?"

Yevul stood there for several seconds before nodding. "Yes, with the hundred most powerful singers, we can be ready tomorrow."

"Good. By the time the sun sets tomorrow, we will begin our assault on Goalton."

CHAPTER 12

Radek had been around elves for nearly two years. He had studied their magic, for all the good that had done, for almost that entire time. Elven masters had tried to train him. He thought he understood enough about elven magic that he couldn't be overly surprised by it, but nothing had prepared him for the sheer *presence* of the most powerful singers on Droshala.

When Meelvania, the first of the hundred to arrive, stepped off her shuttle, the air around her shimmered, as if distorted by heat. Sweat broke out on Radek's brow, and his face felt like it was burning. For a moment, he thought his hair would catch on fire. There was a faint musical sound as she passed, and though it vanished from Radek's mind almost as soon as it entered, it gave him the impression of a forest fire. She gave Radek a level look but didn't stop. She left the hanger bay without a word.

"She's…" Radek's throat was dry, and his skin felt like it would crack. "She's a fire singer."

Ovian nodded. "The best one on the planet. They say she once won an argument with a volcano."

"I didn't think elves used that kind of metaphor," Brenna said with a smile that only looked a little forced.

"I wasn't using a metaphor. A volcano started to erupt. She yelled at it, and it stopped."

"You can't be serious."

"Other masters still don't understand how she did it. The best idea is that she somehow drained the heat from the earth, but the power that would take, especially without an extended song is…" He shivered. "It's unbelievable."

"Why is she here instead of out there, helping to fight the war?"

"Fire isn't that effective in space, and goblins have counter magic built into their ships to prevent us from affecting their engines directly. She has been on a few ground missions, though."

"Ash Bringer," Brenna said, almost under her breath. When the others looked at her, her face darkened. "My mother has heard reports about her. Some of the troops reported one elf turning squadrons of Necal and goblins to ash. She always assumed it to be an exaggeration and that it had to be a group of elven singers or that they had been caught out in the open by a ship or something. It was her, though, wasn't it?"

Ovian nodded. "There are maybe one or two others that could do it, but yes, if there wasn't a bone mage to counter her, she could destroy hundreds of them." He shook his head and laughed. "A bone mage. It would normally take two or three."

"And there are a hundred others like her?" Radek asked.

Ovian shook his head. "She's maybe the third or fourth most powerful singer on the planet. Most of the others aren't nearly as strong, but…"

"They are the hundred most powerful magic users of a race that teaches magic to their children from the time they're old enough to walk," Radek said.

"Before, actually," Ovian said. "We teach babies a type of

emotional projection so that their mothers know if they're hurt or just hungry."

"You teach babies magic?"

Ovian looked up. "Just a little. It's not like it's a hard spell."

Radek and Brenna both stared at him before Radek let out a breath and shook his head. They sat down to wait for the next singer, though Radek thought the docking bay held the faint smell of burnt wood after the fire singer left.

In the end, they spent nearly three hours in the docking bay as transport ships landed, waiting to greet the arriving singers. Radek had to be careful and reign in his mystic senses. Even so, encountering so many powerful singers left his skin tingling, and he found himself breathing faster.

Not all of them were as proud as Meelvania, but they all carried the same air of power. Some were rude. Others would have been happy to spend all day talking with a human shaper, especially one who had dealt with dragon magic. However, even the singers that stopped to talk were soon pulled away by one elven official or another. One elf with pale skin and red eyes made the air around him so cold that Radek thought he could feel ice crystals forming in the back of his throat. The singer moved past them without a word. He kept his eyes forward and glided across the ground, barely seeming to touch it.

"A cold singer?" Radek asked.

Ovian shook his head. "Bayeal is a necromancer."

Radek perked up. "Death magic?"

"Radek no. He draws death to himself. I've heard of people being driven mad just by being near him for too long."

"You're exaggerating," Brenna said.

"Like your mother's scouts exaggerated about Ash Bringer? Ovian asked. "Come on. He was the last one. Do you want to watch them empowering the gem?"

A day ago, Radek wouldn't have hesitated, but that had been before he had been so humbled by seeing so many powerful elven singers. He had encountered strong magic before. He'd once seen a battle between the sea gods Tiamat and Bahamut, but that had been wild and nearly uncontrolled. These singers not only had power, but they had a control over it that only centuries of mastery could grant them. Being close to all of them while they performed a powerful working would be terrifying, but still…

"I'll probably never get another chance to see something like this. Let's go."

CHAPTER 13

Radek had been awed by each of the hundred he had encountered, but as they stood together, their combined power threatened to overwhelm him. More than that, they didn't even gather on a tree. Rather, Yevul and Rania had picked a grove on the ground that somehow amplified elven magic. His skin felt too tight on his body, and everything tingled. He took several deep breaths and had to lean on one of the great trees to avoid falling over.

In the center of the grove, the Hope Diamond sat in the grass, glowing periodically. An elven starfighter stood above it, with tendrils of power emanating from the crystal and wrapping around the vessel. The hundred singers stood in a circle around the ship and diamond.

"I had no idea this kind of power existed." His voice was barely above a whisper.

Ovian nodded, and even Brenna seemed a little uneasy. Then, the elves started to sing.

Once before, he had managed to separate his consciousness from his body as he battled the evil wizard Derek. He had been outmatched then, and it had only been with the aid of Rania that he had managed to survive. This was like that times a thousand. It was like Radek had been plunged into a river of pure magic as the sensations from his body disappeared. Magic was all he could feel. It was all there was. He wanted to reach out and touch it, to hold on to it. He wasn't arrogant enough to think he could do anything with it, no more than a man could control the ocean by swimming in it, but he wanted to feel it around him. He needed it.

"No!"

The word was like thunder in his ears, drowning out even the sense of magic. He looked around and realized he wasn't in the grove anymore. Rather, he was surrounded by darkness, though he could see his own body. The shock brought him back to himself, though he could still feel longing for the magic. After several seconds, he managed a single word.

"What?

Radek wasn't sure if he had spoken out loud or not, but the voice heard him.

"Do not attempt this, Radek."

There was a sense of absolute authority in the voice, and it drove back the longing even further.

"Rania?"

"You are nowhere near ready to handle this kind of power. Stay and observe if you wish, but do not try to interfere."

"Well, isn't this interesting?"

The words washed over Radek like a wave of ice. The voice was like sandpaper rubbing against rock. He gasped, remembering when he encountered Derek in just such a situation. Radek tried to bring his power to bear, to call up his defenses, but in this place that was not a place, trying to reach his power amidst the magic of so many others was like trying to pull oil out of water. The voice laughed, but it wasn't the evil laughter of the traitor wizard. It seemed almost friendly, at least as friendly as a disembodied voice speaking to him in a landscape composed of his own mind could be.

"Have no fear, young human. I am not your enemy. I merely sensed two powerful spirits conversing nearby, and I was curious. I will withdraw. Lady Rania, Ambassador Radek, I hope you forgive the intrusion."

"Of course, Singer Bayeal," Rania said.

The voice gave the impression of bowing its head. Then, it was gone from Radek's senses. For a moment, Radek was speechless.

"Bayeal?" he asked. "That was the necromancer? He could hear us?"

"Did you really believe we could converse like this so near to a necromancer of Bayeal's caliber and that he would not sense us?"

"What do you mean converse like this? I have no idea how we're talking."

"Truly? Well, that is interesting."

"Why?"

"Because this is very advanced magic. It's a strength of humans, in fact."

Radek blinked. "You mean I'm using human magic?"

Though he couldn't see it, Radek had the distinct impression that the voice smirked at him. "Of course. How else would you be doing this?"

Radek paused. He had never considered that. He had always seen his power as an extension of the power of other races, but as Rania had said, he had never been particularly skilled at it. This sort of thing, while not easy, had certainly been simpler than conjuring whirlwinds or carving runes in clay, and if Bayeal sensed them, then this had to be a branch of death magic.

"How…"

Before he could say anything else, the power around him pulsed and shifted. The darkness trembled, and he felt himself being caught up in it, but the voice, Rania, held him down.

"Release your power, Radek. It is far too dangerous for you to meddle with."

Radek nodded, and with an effort, he forced himself back into his body. He swooned and placed a hand on a nearby tree. He focused on the roughness of the bark until he could steady himself. Brenna was staring at him.

"Who were you talking to?"

"Rania," Radek said, "and Bayeal, apparently."

Ovian, who had been staring at the singing mages, turned to stare at him.

"Bayeal?" He looked back at the pale elf. Like the rest, Bayeal was singing, though Radek couldn't make out his voice. Before Ovian could say anything else, the singing changed tones, and the hairs on Radek's arms stood on end. Though he couldn't remember them after they had been sung, Elven songs always left him with the impression of being pleasant. These notes, however, were harsh, and he found himself covering his ears with his hands. Ovian and Brenna were doing the same thing. Even some of the singers swayed, but none of them stopped. The gem in the center of the grove took on an azure glow, and the trees bent away from it. After a few seconds, it emitted a light so bright it hurt to look at. Radek could sense the growing power within. It was so much as to be unimaginable. No crystal, especially not one as small as the one in the center of the grove, could hold so much power, but yet, as the elves sang, the jewel which had once been called the Hope Diamond, glowed brighter still. A thing like heat, but that Radek could only detect with his mystical awareness, drove him back with its intensity.

"Now!"

Radek thought the voice was Rania's, but he was so distracted by the power that he couldn't be sure. The jewel flashed a blinding blue, and when the light faded, the ship was gone. The jewel glittered in the afternoon sun, a magnificent specimen, but it no longer glowed with the light of unimaginable power.

"Did it work?" Ovian called out.

A few of the mages looked over to them, but none said a word. Instead, they started talking amongst themselves. It was only when Yevul cleared his throat that the closest mages went silent. Slowly, the wave of quiet spread until it covered everyone. Yevul tapped his wrist communicator, and the air above it shimmered, projecting the message he had just received. It was a map of the sector, with two dots flashing. One was Droshala, while the other was some uninhabited world, thirteen lightyears away.

"I have just received confirmation that the craft arrived after thirty-five seconds. All living matter is intact as well. I think we can call this test a complete success. Everyone get some rest. I want to be able to do it again tomorrow. Before the sun sets here, we will be at Goalton."

CHAPTER 14

Thirty-seven capital ships, fifty-three midsized cruisers, and nearly two hundred starfighters, including the ones brought by Rania, made the most impressive fleet Radek had ever seen. That much power was enough to reduce a planet to dust. Of course, Goalton would have defenses of its own, but Radek doubted it would be enough to counter all of this, even if they had something like a nova dragon or a ring ship.

They all gathered around the *Linala*, an elven heavy cruiser. Aside from the *Linala*, every elven vessel was completely powered down to avoid interfering with the magic. The dragon ships, having been constructed using different principles, would protect their elven counterparts once they arrived for the few seconds it took them to power up, while dwarven and merfolk vessels would begin the attack.

"I didn't think I would be so nervous," Ovian said. "I don't even know why. I've gone into battle before."

"But we've never *planned* to go into battle before," Radek said. "Especially with so many others. For us, it always just sort of happened. That makes a difference, I think."

"There is a buildup of power coming from the *Linala*," *Wind* said.

"How soon until we enter hyperspace?" Brenna asked.

"Approximately fifteen minutes."

"So long?" Radek asked. "The test happened so quickly."

"The power has to spread out, and that's not easy to do without losing the integrity of the spell," Ovian said. "Fifteen minutes is actually really fast."

Radek spent the next little while going over *Wind*'s systems, more because he couldn't think of anything else to do than for any other reason. Everything ran at a hundred percent. What little damage they had sustained in the battle had long since been taken care of by *Wind*'s self-repair mechanism. Finally, he told the ship to examine its own programming. He didn't know enough about dragon programming to be sure, but he thought he detected the changes Rania had mentioned.

As he tried to understand what he'd done, he found himself getting hot. He wiped sweat from his brow, and his heart pounded inside his chest. His skin tingled, and it took him a minute to recognize it as the warmth of elven magic. He looked toward the heavy cruiser, but though he knew that was where the magic came from, he couldn't tell that with his senses. It was as Ovian had said. The power spread out like a wave that had washed over him and left him completely immersed. The magic was everywhere. It filled every inch of him. He tapped *Wind*'s screen, switching to the short-range sensor, but like Radek's own senses, the viewscreen only indicated the entire area was suffused with magic.

"*Wind*," Brenna said, "what are these readings? They don't make sense. They say this goes on forever."

"Not forever," *Wind* said. "The veil is too thick to be pierced by my sensors."

"It's like if you have a blindfold on," Ovian said. "All you can see is the cloth, but that doesn't mean all the world is cloth."

Radek gaped. "How thick does magic have to be to do that?"

"In order to completely wash out my sensors, it would have to be at least three hundred diads."

Radek looked to Ovian, who made an exaggerated motion of rolling his eyes. Radek let out a long breath. "Never mind. I probably wouldn't understand your explanation anyway. How much longer until we go?"

Before *Wind* could answer, space peeled away, revealing the whiteness of hyperspace. Radek almost screamed as the feel of magic was ripped away. His vision blurred, and for a moment, he thought he would fall over. After a few seconds, however, the world cleared. *Wind*'s sensors revealed they were going at an almost unbelievable speed.

"Radek, are you okay?" Brenna asked.

Radek blinked and looked over his shoulder at her. It took a few seconds for everything to stop shaking. She wore a worried expression, but he nodded. "I think so. I just need a few minutes to rest."

"We don't have a few minutes." She tapped her viewscreen a few times. "*Wind*, give me directional control."

"Do it," Radek said.

Wind beeped in acknowledgement, and the light in the control sphere dimmed a little. Radek leaned back as they popped back into existence. *Wind* turned sharply, and an arrow-shaped goblin ship came into view. Ovian touched the firing control. A spray of blue balls of energy shot forward. They splashed against the enemy shields for a second. Then, the shields winked out as the ship went up in a ball of flame. *Wind*'s own shields flashed into visibility before the ship darted to one side. By then, Radek had recovered, but he didn't dare take control from Brenna in the middle of a battle. Instead, he kept an eye on the proximity sensors.

Wind's alarms blared. Radek increased the range of the sensors and saw that a capital ship had a lock on them. Brenna turned toward it. Radek screamed as it fired a laser blast at them. Rather than swerve out of the way. Brenna altered their course only slightly. The shields shimmered, and the ship rocked as the blast hit them. When it faded, Radek switched the screen to a status display. He gasped.

"Shields went down only half a percent."

"I knew it would work," Brenna said, pressing forward. The goblin ship grew in front of them.

"You knew what would work?" Ovian asked.

"I angled the shield so the blast bounced off of it."

"Wouldn't it be easier to just avoid it?" Radek asked.

"Yes, but then we wouldn't be here."

Radek looked forward and cried out. There were less than a hundred yards from the ship. They were close enough that he could make out individual goblins through the windows. Brenna jerked them to one side. They missed the goblin ship by inches. As soon as they were passed it, *Wind* spun in space so fast that they would have been crushed against their seats if not for the advanced inertial dampeners. The engine exhaust filled their vision. Ovian fired, but they were moving too fast, and soon, the ship was out of their sight.

"We barely disabled the engines." Ovian was almost pouting.

"That's all we were supposed to do."

"It was?"

Brenna turned toward another large ship, though this one faced away from them. "Weren't you even listening at the briefing?"

Ovian hesitated. He looked at Radek and smiled. "Not really."

"We're not supposed to spend too much time on any one ship. We'll just disable them and leave them for the others to mop up."

"What others?"

The goblin vessels went up in a flash of light. Radek looked at the sensors and laughed. A merfolk capital ship. Bubble ships were incredibly powerful with weapons that had more destructive potential than any race save the dragons themselves. Unfortunately, they were also filled with water, and the added mass made it so that they usually lacked the maneuverability other races possessed. Of course, that wasn't a problem when a capital ship had been disabled. The goblin ships scattered as the dragon-built vessels broke away to pursue them. A number of other enemies had been disabled, and the merfolk ships tore through them.

Like many of the others, Radek had been worried that the goblins would learn of this attack. If they had, however, they hadn't had the time to prepare. Space was filled with exploding goblin ships. *Wind's* alarms blared in an almost constant tone, indicating that they had been locked on to. Brenna piloted her with amazing skill, however, and no ship could maintain a lock for more than a second. More than once, Brenna was able to bring an enemy into sight to be picked off by Ovian. There were just so many of them, though. They had been surprised, but they were quickly regrouping.

Goblin weapons splashed against *Wind's* shields, and half a dozen dragon vessels had been disabled. Elves deployed to guard them. Before *Wind* could do anything to help, three ships locked onto them. Brenna turned sharply, and two of them lost their lock. One of the indicators went red. Brenna uttered something in dwarven as the ship went through several sharp turns, but it did no good. A missile slammed into *Wind*. Rather than a normal explosion, however, sickly green energy seemed to wrap around them. Shield power plummeted, and Radek felt the cold power of goblin bone magic. He hit a button on a panel, disabling the shields. They winked out, and the spell fizzled away. A blast shook them as it hit their hull. Some of their systems went offline, but Radek didn't spare the second it would take to see what they were. He reactivated the shields, though the goblin spell had reduced them to a mere fifteen percent. Another ship locked onto them, but before it could fire, a brilliant flash of blue illuminated space, and the enemy ship exploded.

"The elven fleet has engaged the enemy," *Wind* said.

Ovian sighed and rolled his eyes in the exaggerated way he always acted when making human gestures. "It's about time."

In a matter of seconds, the goblin counter-attack had been turned back. None of the Vanelian ships had been destroyed, though a number had been damaged. Fortunately, most of those were the dragon vessels which had sophisticated self-repair systems. *Wind* had been damaged as well, though she would be better in few hours.

The *Linala* had come through the battle with only minor damage and sent out a signal for the attack's various leaders to dock with them. Brenna directed *Wind* to the heavy cruiser, but they had only covered half the distance when *Wind*'s proximity sensors went off. Radek glanced at the screen, and his eyes went wide.

"*Wind*, is that what I think it is?"

Wind's avatar appeared on the screen and inclined her head. "A ring ship. They are hailing the *Linala* on an open channel."

"Put it on screen," Radek said.

A gray-skinned man with eyes that looked like diamonds appeared. "General Verren, this is Gold Yanelen of the ship *Kenilan*, at your service."

"*Wind*," Brenna said, "are there clan markings on that ship?"

Twin hammers appeared on the screen, and Brenna laughed. "Those belong to the Rune Blood, one of the shipbuilder clans."

Radek blinked. "You mean…"

"The Runestone Fleet has built a ring ship!"

CHAPTER 15

Radek and his friends followed the dwarf who had met them at the docking bay through a series of corridors. It was eerie for him to walk through the halls of the ring ship and not be worried about being found out by the Necal, the rebel dwarves who had built the last ring ship. There were more than a few differences, though. This ship was significantly cleaner, and there were no workers wearing goblin slave collars. Dwarves they passed stopped and stared in a way that made Radek a little uneasy, and he did his best to ignore it. As they walked, they were joined by other leaders of the attacking fleet who had docked at different bays. One of the last ones was the human form of Rania, who was constantly looking around with wide-eyed awe. She glared at him.

"Did you aid with this?"

"Me? What makes you think I did?"

"Because they have managed to combined dwarven, goblin, and dragon magic. That requires the abilities of a shaper."

"Not exactly, my lady," one of the dwarves said. When Rania turned her gaze at him, he shrank back. He looked to his companions for support before speaking again. "We were part of the force that rescued Silver Balena's daughter and her friends when they destroyed the first ring ship. Once that operation was done, we went back to Idella Vulan for a salvage operation. We were able to delve into the gas giant and retrieve certain elements of the original ring ship. It's taken us a year to repair the components and incorporate them into our design." He bowed at Radek. "We would, of course, welcome the ambassador's aid. Our efforts have been far from perfect."

Rania sniffed, though she allowed herself the faintest hint of a smile.

"Impressive. I can't speak to the interface between the magics, but the dragon magic seems strong."

The gathered generals and leaders whispered to each other. Radek caught a couple of them asking who this was, and he realized that most didn't know the dragon could take a humanoid form. Radek was trying to think of a tactful way to say that when their dwarf guide led them into a large room.

In spite of being on a ship, the room had a stone floor and walls. The image of a hammer had been engraved on the wall opposite the door and seemed to dominate the room. Radek thought he could feel the faint hint of dwarven magic coming from it. An obsidian table sat in the middle with a chair for every person present. Yanelen sat at the head of the table and motioned for the rest to join them. However, no sooner had they done so, than General Verren got to his feet again and scowled.

"When were you going to tell us you had a ring ship?"

The dwarf laughed. "When we were certain it worked. This ship is amazing."

Verren's annoyance was mirrored on the faces of most of the other leaders, but that was slowly fading as the implications of a ship like this fully dawned on everyone.

"How quickly can it build?" Radek asked.

"If it doesn't have to gather resources, it can build a squadron a day. A capital cruiser can be done in three, but we've been focusing on smaller ships."

"Why?"

He smirked. "Because we don't have the plans for a dragon-designed capital ship."

"You mean you've gotten this ship to build dragon starfighters?"

"A variant using rune magic. They lack your vessel's artificial intelligence and a few other features, but yes, they are quite effective."

"We need to reevaluate our plans," General Verren said. "With this new resource, we should revise our tactics."

Yanelen shook his head. "As I understand it, your plan depends on a rapid strike. You don't have time to revise it before the bulk of the goblins arrive to defend Goalton."

"Then you just came to show off your new ring ship without intended to let us use it?"

"We're here in case the goblins throw something at you that you're not expecting and to provide back up."

"But surely we can come up with a better use…"

Alarms blared, and Yanelen pressed buttons that had been concealed in the table. Above them, an image of Goalton appeared with several dots beeping. A status display appeared in front of Radek and the rest. Dozens of ships rose from the surface. Brenna tapped the screen, and more information appeared. Radek's blood went cold. They didn't appear to be as advanced as *Wind*, but there was no doubt where the design had come from.

"Those were built from dragon technology."

CHAPTER 16

Radek ran through the halls, not waiting for a dwarf to guide him. Experience had taught them that losing contact with *Wind* could be disastrous, so they'd had the elves sing a communication spell allowing them to keep in constant contact. The starfighter still had the designs for the last ring ship, and she guided them to the docking bay where she waited. The bay was a flurry of activity. *Wind* wasn't the only ship docked there. There were a number of vessels that Radek had originally thought were purely dwarven but that he could now recognize as influenced by dragon design. Dwarves scrambled to get in, and Radek found himself anxious to see what these new ships could do in battle. They ran up to *Wind,* and she lowered her hatch to allow them in. The ship's engine had started before they were halfway up, and they were in the air as soon as they had sat down. The dwarven ships may have been influenced by dragon design, but they were not dragon ships, and *Wind* zipped out of the docking bay before any of the other ships had finished powering up.

The battle was already underway. This time, it was the Vanellian ships that had been caught off guard. There hadn't been enough time for the more heavily damaged dragon ships to repair themselves, and they had suffered the brunt of the attack. Fully half of their more advanced vessels had been destroyed. The remaining ones had managed to get in an elven battle formation and were doing an admirable job of holding their own, but they were outnumbered at least three to one. The remaining elven and merfolk ships were providing support, and already, dozens of other ships streamed out of the dwarven ring ship.

The goblin ships turned to meet the new foes. Missiles shot forward from the dwarven vessels. *Wind*'s sensors beeped when they exploded. Radek's eyes went wide as he examined the energy signatures.

"*Wind*, are those what I think they are?"

"Stellar core missiles."

"How could they duplicate those? I thought they needed dragon magic."

"The gold magic principles they employ are not overly complicated. They can be duplicated with rune magic, especially if done by a master."

"Are they as good as yours?" Ovian asked.

More of the missiles exploded against a dozen goblin vessels. Half were destroyed outright, while the others had shields disabled. The nearby elven ships opened fire, and the goblins went up in a series of explosions.

"Yes," *Wind* said. "They appear to be as effective."

There were only a few goblin ships left by that point. *Wind*'s avatar periodically gave status reports until the sky was clear of enemies. No sooner had the last goblin ship exploded than *Wind*'s face faded, replaced by General Verren. "Well done, everyone. Return to the ring ship. We have much to discuss and not a lot of time to do it in."

They headed for the docking bay, and the three disembarked. The halls were full of discussion about how effective the dwarven force had been. Radek was about to enter the conference room when a voice spoke from the shadows in a tone that made the hairs on the back of his neck stand on end.

"Ambassador Radek, may I have a word?"

He stopped and stared as others moved around then. Many threw uneasy looks at the corner. It took him a few seconds to see the tall figure. It stepped out of the shadows without making a sound. Radek thought it was a human at first, but he had pale red eyes, and his face had the angular features of an elf, though he stood at least a foot taller than any elf he had ever seen. The pointed teeth that showed when he smiled were definitely not elven, nor was the musty smell that filled the air. Ovian hissed, and Brenna just gaped at him.

"Yes?"

"I am Stregoi of the Shadows."

"You're a dhampir," Ovian said.

Stregoi inclined his head. "As I said, I am of the shadows."

"What's a dhampir?" Radek asked.

"A part vampire," Ovian said.

"How can somebody be a part vampire?" Ort asked.

Stregoi's face became expressionless. "The same way someone can be part human or part elf." He gave himself a small shrug. "There hasn't been a true vampire for almost five hundred years, and the truth is that we have no idea how they first bred with living beings. Since then, however, we can have children just like anyone else."

"What do you want?" Radek asked, uncomfortably aware of the leaders of the compact passing him by.

"I heard from the elf Yevul. He told me that you have an interest in learning death magic."

Radek stared at him. He then looked to Ovian, who was shaking his head. Brenna just looked confused. Radek had always thought that death magic was just like any other element, something like water or air. Some races might be better at it than others, but every race could, for example, learn to throw a ball of fire or call a blast of wind. On the other hand, if anyone would know a lot about death magic, it would be a part vampire. He nodded to his friends. "You guys go ahead. I'm going to stay."

Ovian grabbed his sleeve. "Radek, remember what I said about necromancy."

Radek shook his head. "We need it."

Ovian opened his mouth to argue, but Brenna put a hand on his shoulder and shook her head. He seemed to deflate and allowed her to lead him into the conference room. Radek looked to the half-vampire and nodded. "How do we start?"

The man motioned for him to follow, and Radek fell into step behind him. The shadows seemed to stretch out to cover him as they walked, and his steps echoed on the metallic floor. Stregoi led him to a small room that looked like it might have been built for storage. It had been emptied, though it still held the faintly oily scent common to all dwarven constructs.

"Your friend spoke to you about the dangers of the magic of the dead?" Radek nodded, and Stregoi went on. "I very much doubt that he knows more than the barest fragment of the true dangers I have to deal with. Make no mistake. This can destroy you."

"But you're going to teach me?"

"If a shaper on the front lines of a war with goblins wishes to employ death magic against them, I have no objection, but the question is if you actually know what death magic is."

"Spirits," Radek said. "Something to do with them, anyway."

Stregoi's red eyes focused on Radek, and the temperature in the room seemed to drop several degrees. He told himself that he had faced greater dangers than this man, but that thought didn't stop his heart from racing nor his brow from practically dripping sweat. Finally, the necromancer let out a breath.

"The magic of death is the magic of worlds, this world and the spirit world. In some ways, it's related to time since spirits are linked to the past. At its basic level, it can affect creatures such as me as well as incorporeal beings like ghosts. It can be used to communicate spirit to spirit, and powerful applications of it can even affect the souls of living beings."

Radek opened his mouth to speak but closed it again. Stregoi smiled. He raised a gnarled finger and pointed it at Radek.

"Go ahead and ask your question. You won't be able to think straight until you ask it anyway."

"Can you bring back the dead?"

He shook his head. "The dead are gone, Radek, and there are some lines even I cannot cross. Sometimes, a particularly powerful ghost can inhabit the living, though never for long. Any body but its own will eventually reject a spirit. Even one's own body becomes unsuitable a few minutes after death. No, I'm sorry. We can see spirits. We can talk to them. We can even bring back a semblance of life, but it is not truly them, not in any way that matters."

Radek perked up. "We can talk to them?"

"Some, but it is not as easy as most assume. Finding a specific spirit can be difficult. Not all spirits linger, and even those that do usually pass on eventually."

"Can you find my father?"

Stregoi was shaking his head before Radek finished speaking. "I knew you would ask, so I looked for him already. Your father died almost two years ago, fifty light-years away. He had no connection to this war or to Goalton. If his spirit lingered, it would have been on *Vanel*, and I doubt that any of the station's spirits lingered after it was destroyed, if any existed there at all." Radek looked away, but Stregoi kept speaking. "Don't feel bad about that. Spirits linger only when they have something keeping them here. It is not a pleasant existence. If there were any spirits aboard *Vanel*, they would no doubt be grateful about being able to move on." He put a hand on Radek's shoulder. "For what it's worth, I believe that if your father was ever a ghost, he passed on long before the station was destroyed."

Radek blinked. "Why do you think that?"

"Because the only thing that would hold him to this world is you. You have saved the galaxy more than once. No one, spirit or otherwise, could truly believe that you needed someone to look after you."

Radek bit his lips but nodded. "How do we start?"

***

By the end of the lesson, Radek was shivering. Death magic had a peculiar coldness to it that had nothing to do with temperature. Several times, he thought he heard voices, and once, Radek was sure he could sense Stregoi's soul within him. Learning about death magic felt oddly familiar to Radek. Once he was done with the lesson, he mentioned it to Stregoi. The Dhampir nodded.

"Of course. As your friend said, I am part vampire, but I have more than a little human blood in me. The magic that I taught you is based on human magic."

Radek stared at him. So many questions ran through his mind, but he couldn't think of what else to ask. The lesson had been exhausting. Stregoi seemed to understand. "Your first exposure to this type of magic can be draining on both the soul and the body. Get some rest. I'll be happy to answer your questions in the morning."

CHAPTER 17

The meeting was over long before Radek was done with his lesson, but his friends were waiting for him. Quarters had been prepared for them aboard the *Linala*, but Radek was exhausted, and in the end, they all got quarters aboard the ring ship. He felt like he had barely laid down when his door dinged at him.

At first, he didn't respond, but it dinged again and again. Finally, he blinked the sleep away. He rolled out of bed and stretched a little to work out the stiffness in his body before opening the door. Ovian was there and grabbed Radek's hand, practically dragging him out of the room. Brenna was waiting down the hall.

"What is it?"

"He's back."

"Who?"

Ovian looked upward. "Yevul. Weren't you even listening in the meeting?"

Radek gave him a level stare. "I wasn't at the meeting, remember?"

Brenna smirked at the elf. "Weren't you paying attention?" Ovian rolled his eyes, but she turned to Radek. "Yevul went down to Goalton to see if he could provide us with any information, but he only left a few hours ago."

Ovian nodded. "He's very good. He insisted you be there when he told us what he found."

"What could he have found in a few hours that would be important enough for him to come back so quickly?" Radek asked.

"Something that makes us have to advance our timetable."

Radek jumped at the voice behind him. He turned to see Yevul standing a few feet away. He wore a stoic face and moved past them without making a sound. Dried mud crusted off his cloak, releasing a sour odor. Radek and his friends exchanged glances before following.

Yevul moved like a shadow. He hardly seemed to breathe. He ghosted into the room and sat down to wait for the rest of the leaders. It took nearly half an hour for the rest of them to fly over from the *Linala*, but the spy retained his cold silence the entire time.

"Yevul," Verren said once the others had arrived, "I've never been a fan of your dramatic gestures. Would you care to tell me why you woke us all up in the middle of the night?"

"Because you need to lead a strike on the goblin shipyards as soon as possible with as much strength as is available. Don't wait until morning."

Verren stood up, his face red with anger. "What? We have a timetable. We have a plan. We can't just upend that because you say so."

"Your plan needs to change, or this war will be lost by the end of the week. They didn't build a ring ship. They constructed ground-based shipyards. They're building dragon ships down there."

"We know that," Gold Yanelen said. "We fought a squadron of them yesterday."

"You fought a squadron of starfighters. They are building nova dragons. At least one that I found. Possibly more. If you don't stop them, Droshala, Earth, Cruska, and Avuana could be destroyed before we could react."

Verren's mouth seemed frozen open. For a moment, he just stared at Yevul. "Nova dragons?" He turned to Radek and Ovian. "You two destroyed a nova dragon before."

Radek shook his head at remembering the battle. "We destroyed an old ship that wasn't fully functional by sabotaging the hyperdrive. I don't think we'll get a chance like that again."

"We have a fleet of dragon ships, though," Verren said. "That has to mean something."

"Yes, a fleet of *Stellar Wind* type ships could eventually destroy a dreadnaught," Rania said. "It would not be an easy battle, but it could be done. There would be no guarantee it could be done before one of your homeworlds is destroyed, however. I believe Yevul is correct. If this threat is to be stopped, it should be done before the dreadnaughts are operational."

"The first will be able to launch any day now," Yevul said. "If one of them gets off Goalton, we'll have to go after it, and that will mean breaking the siege. We won't get another chance like this, and you know it. That only leaves one choice."

One by one, the leaders of the fleet nodded. Even General Verren accepted it without comment. Dragon dreadnaughts, or nova dragons as they were more commonly called, were the deadliest ships to ever fly through the stars. Their primary weapons could destroy entire planets. Just one could shift the balance of power in the galaxy. More than one would deliver all of them into goblin hands. Yevul was right. If the goblins had that kind of firepower, there was only one thing they could do. Gold Yanelen turned to Yevul.

"We will be ready to strike within the hour."

Intool, the merfolk ambassador, nodded. "I believe my forces would be best suited for an orbital bombardment."

"Agreed," Verren said. "I'll head back to the *Linala* and prepare our fighters. Yevul, provide us all with the relevant information and give us any sensor data you may have gathered. We will scan the planet for any other possible sites. It will take me more than an hour to organize it all, but not much. We will depart in two hours."

CHAPTER 18

"Can they really do that?" Radek asked. "Build nova dragons?"

Rania tapped her viewscreen, and a hologram appeared in the air in front of it. The ax-shaped vessel rotated and seemed to fire as it turned toward Radek. The sight made goosebumps run up his arms. Rania nodded, her emerald hair bouncing. They were in her quarters, which contained only a bed that would be barely large enough for her humanoid form. She didn't seem to mind the starkness, though.

"We have seen plenty of evidence that they have dragon aid. Not many of us knew how to construct dreadnaughts, but there were a few. Grr'ink'itor was a weapon specialist. It is not impossible that he knew enough to construct a vessel, albeit imperfectly."

"But aren't all the power sources in Treya's sun?" Ovian asked. "How could they build a ship without those?"

Rania spread her fingers. The holographic ship zoomed in until they were looking at one of the interior chambers. The spherical reactor in the center glowed with a golden light as Rania spoke. "They may have been able to construct more, or these ships may be fueled by a different power source. The shaper Derek may have been able to come up with something before his death."

"Is there any way to detect where those power sources are?" Radek asked, trying to avoid shivering at the name of the traitor human. "At least if we destroy those, we could stop them from having full access to their systems."

"It is possible," Rania said, "but if Yevul is correct and they are ready to launch, it is likely that they already have the power source installed."

"All right. If that's not an option, then we'll all join the attack."

Rania raised an eyebrow. "You have grown comfortable with me, but I did not realize that extended to you giving me commands."

Radek's blood went cold. "I'm sorry. I didn't mean…"

Rania laughed, and though it might have been Radek's imagination, he thought he saw a fiery glow in her mouth, and he smelled smoke. "Give it no mind, Radek. I pledged myself to your aid, and I do not take offense at words like that from friends."

Radek blinked. "Friends?"

The dragon smiled. "Of course, though I admit, I never thought to call such short-lived beings friends, but I cannot think of any word that is more accurate."

Radek grinned and inclined his head. Then, on impulse, he extended his hand. For several seconds, Rania just stared at it, and Radek began to worry that he had made a mistake. Just as he was about to take it back, however, she took it and shook once. Then, she walked out the door, and they followed her to the docking bay where *Wind* was. She reached the center of the bay and took on a brilliant golden glow. Her form seemed to become fluid. A heartbeat later, a dragon flew out of the atmosphere shield. Brenna smiled widely.

"I don't think I'm ever going to get tired of seeing that."

Radek nodded, but Ovian was already running to *Wind*. He was in his seat before the other two even started heading toward the ship, and as they entered, he grinned.

"What took you so long?"

Radek glared at him. He was about to take the control sphere when he paused. He looked over his shoulder. "Brenna, you take the controls."

She blinked. "What? Me?"

Radek nodded. "You're better at it than I am." He bit his lower lip and tried to sound like it didn't bother him. "You can take my seat. I think the control sphere would be more responsive."

She just stared at him for several seconds. Finally, she shook her head. "I've been working through the console this whole time. It's probably better not to change that up right now."

Radek turned back and brought up sensor data. *Wind* lifted into the air and shot out of the docking bay. They joined a squadron of other dragon fighters, which formed up around them. There hadn't been enough time for the more severely damaged ships to repair themselves, and with those that had been destroyed, they were only left with a quarter of their original force. Even that, however, would have been more than a match for most fleets before the war. Added to that, once they joined with the forces off the dwarven ring ship, they had a fighting force unequaled since the days the dragons roamed the stars openly.

Coordinates flashed on their screen courtesy of Yevul. Radek read over the plan and took a deep breath. Gold Yanelen had scanned the planet and had discovered three other sites that were probably shipyards, but the decision was made to attack the one Yevul had found first. They didn't know how well defended they were, so General Verren wanted to throw everything they had at their first target. *Wind* and the rest of the attack fleet tilted forward and rushed into the atmosphere of Goalton.

CHAPTER 19

W*ind* had never entered an atmosphere at combat speeds before, and Radek hadn't expected it to be so rough. The ship rocked, and the shields popped into existence as their strength dropped ten percent within seconds. Immediately, it started to recover, though. Sensors indicated all ships had suffered similar damage, none of it serious, and by the time they reached the first shipyard, most had recovered completely.

"Ovian, fire," Brenna said.

"Where is it?" Ovian asked, staring at the empty field before them.

"Do you ever read the mission briefings?" Brenna asked.

"Why do you ask when you know I don't?"

The ground was getting uncomfortably close, but neither of them seemed to be paying attention to that. Radek reached for the control sphere but stopped himself. He trusted Brenna. He repeated that to himself as the ground got closer and closer.

"The shipyard is underground. Fire the plasma beam cannon!"

"Why would they build them underground?" Ovian asked, though he was already firing.

The beam turned the earth into molten rock. Sensors indicated they had melted through nearly fifty feet of dirt and stone when Brenna shouted again.

"Stellar core missile!"

This time, Ovian didn't hesitate. A missile shot forward, splashing against lava and sinking in. A second later, an explosion rocked the earth. A shower of dirt and rock flew into the sky and splashed into the shields of several of the lowest flying ships. Others fired as well, filling the air with a cloud of red dust. It cleared after a few seconds. Beneath them was a huge cavern, at least a mile across. Construction equipment was everywhere, though much of it had been wrecked. At the very center of the cavern, amidst a few squadrons of lesser vessels, was a silvery ship as big as a couple of buildings and shaped vaguely like an ax. It gave Radek the chills. He tapped his screen to get more information. Yevul had been right. This ship was nearly complete. Ovian saw it too, because immediately, two stellar core missiles shot forward. They impacted the hull, and Radek let out a breath of relief that the shields weren't on. The missiles hit, collapsing a small area of the hull. Before they could do anything else, though, *Wind*'s alarms blared, and the vessel shook as a purple beam enveloped them.

Brenna jerked the ship to one side but not before they had lost a quarter of their shield strength. Radek checked the sensors. Goblin ships were inbound while others rushed through the ruined docking bay, trying to find a ship that worked. The first blast had come from a ground-based turret. There was another flash of purple, and an elven fighter went up in a puff of smoke.

"Brenna, Ovian," Radek said.

"I see it," Brenna said as she turned *Wind* toward the turret. Illusion magic had been used to disguise it as a rock, but now that it had fired, it was giving off heat, and *that* they could detect. Ovian fired and a series of blue balls shot forward. As soon as they touched the surface of the rock, it shimmered. A few seconds later, the rock exploded, taking the illusion with it.

"*Wind*, can you find other turrets?" Radek asked.

"My sensors cannot see through the illusions; however, I am capable of detecting the illusions themselves."

"Good enough. Show us. Send the sensor data to the other *Wind*-class ships."

"What about the nova dragon?" Ovian asked.

"It's on the ground and unpowered," Radek said. "The others can take care of it, but those turrets could take down half our attack force."

A dozen other *Wind*-class ships broke off from the main attack, each one targeting a rock or tree. Some of the turrets fired back, but the goblins obviously hadn't expected their weapons to be detected so quickly, and most were caught unaware. In a matter of seconds, their targets had been destroyed, and they moved on to others. The goblins, apparently realizing that their illusions wouldn't help, fired freely with all the remaining turrets. The attacking fleet scattered, targeting the turrets. They weren't heavily defended, relying primarily on their illusions. As a result, the attack fleet made short work of them. While they did, brilliant balls of energy rained down from the sky, launched by the merfolk ships. The entire shipyard became a pool of molten rock and metal. Sensors reported that the air outside had become toxic with the fumes of wrecked ships, and the land had been transformed into a desolate wasteland. There were several explosions before everything went quiet.

"Well, that went well," Ovian said.

"The others won't be so easy," Radek said.

"Why is that?" Ovian asked.

Radek brought up the sensor data. Multiple squadrons of goblin and Necal vessels were heading their way. "Now, they know we're coming."

CHAPTER 20

The next shipyard was only a few miles away. By the time they arrived, the merfolk bombardment had already broken through the ground and eliminated most of the hidden turrets, exposing the shipyard and severely damaging the nova dragon. Some of the goblin ships were heading into orbit, and half of the attacking fleet broke off to defend the merfolk. The rest continued on. Once they reached the third shipyard, however, Radek gasped, and curses came over the comm.

"That's a nova dragon," someone said.

The huge ship was in the air and headed right for them. Sensors detected an energy build up as the dreadnaught prepared to fire.

"The ship is not fully operational," *Wind* said.

"Of course," Brenna said after they had relayed the information to the rest of the fleet. "It may not be finished, but it's still probably one of the strongest ships they have available, especially on such short notice."

"*Wind,* what don't they have finished?"

"Gold drive does not appear to be operational."

"They don't really need that right now. Anything else?"

"Spells to reinforce the hull are not in place."

"How about shields?"

The elven ships fired, but the shield stopped them without apparent damage. The fleet scattered and tried to attack from above, but they inflicted no damage.

"They are fully operational."

"We need twenty stellar core missiles focused on the same spot. Broadcast that to the fleet."

Wind beeped in acknowledgement. "Gold Yanelen does not want to waste that many resources. Their ships do not have molecular fabrication capabilities, and the missiles are apparently quite costly to produce."

"Tell him he has to."

Brenna was already speaking, though. "Gold Yanelen, you will issue those instructions to your fighters."

The dwarven leader's voice came over the comm link. "You are of the iron, are you not?"

The nova dragon fired, and the blast took out three of the elven ships. The *Wind* class vessels were firing as well. The nova dragon's shields were wavering, but they were still at over ninety percent.

"I am aboard the ship that destroyed both the first nova dragon and the first ring ship, flying with the people who did those deeds. You will obey, or I will see that elders of the Rune Blood hear that your insubordination resulted in a nova dragon escaping. See if you are still of the gold after that, assuming Cruska even exists then."

Yanelen uttered something in Dwarven, which made Brenna smile. Both Radek and Ovian were staring at her, but she only shrugged. "Sometimes, the upper ranks can be a little thick-headed. I got through to him."

"But should you really have threatened him like that?" Radek asked.

Before she could answer, nearly two dozen ships launched missiles at the nova dragon. Half of them impacted the shields within ten feet of each other. The rest crashed against the hull in a series of explosions. The nova dragon's engine sputtered. Its shields flashed to visibility before vanishing, and the ship crashed to the earth. General Verren started transmitting orders for the next target when Rania's face appeared on their screen.

"Radek, I require your aid."

"What is it?"

"I have discovered the source of their power. There is a dragon graveyard beneath the surface."

CHAPTER 21

How would a dragon graveyard even get on Goalton?" Radek asked as they pulled away from the rest of the fleet. "Have dragons ever lived on Goalton?"

"Not to my knowledge," Rania said. "So far as I know, no dragon has made a home on any world since we left Earth. I have no idea how they got so many here."

Radek paused. "Are there dragon graveyards on Earth?"

Rania laughed. "We left your world long ago, even by our standards. Any dragon bones that remained would have long ago turned to dust."

"That doesn't answer the original question," Brenna said. She took a deep breath. "Lady Rania, could a group of dragons have settled here?"

Rania's image on the screen huffed, expelling a stream of smoke from her nostrils, which was odd since the image on the screen was nothing more than a projection sent to them directly from Rania's mind. "We are not social creatures. We do not even share stars with each other."

"But you haven't been in contact with other dragons for a long time."

"No."

"So then, it's possible."

"I suppose so. The graveyard is there. They appear to be using the bones to fortify the ground above it. We'll have to walk."

Outside, Rania banked and headed for a low mountain range. There was an isolated ledge that would be practically impossible to get to without flying, and the dragon changed to humanoid form as she landed. *Wind* set down next to her, and they got out. Rania motioned for them to follow and led them into a small opening in the rock. Ovian and Brenna were both shorter than Radek. They could walk upright, but if Radek didn't slouch, he thought he would scrape his head on the hanging stalactites. Rania, whose humanoid form normally stood a foot taller than Radek, had simply changed into a smaller version of herself. Radek winced at the smell of mold and stagnant water, but the others didn't react to it. They hadn't gone too far into it before it became too dark to see. When he mentioned it, Rania seemed surprised, and a ball of golden light appeared over her hand.

"Ah yes. I had forgotten about human vision."

"How did you even find this place?" Radek asked.

"I sensed the death of my own kind as I flew over it."

Radek perked up. "Death magic?"

"After a fashion."

Radek closed his eyes and tried to sense the imprint on the world as Stregoi had shown him. He wasn't sure, but he thought he sensed something, a peculiar cold warmth. He couldn't think of any other way to explain it. He reached out and screamed. He felt like he was on fire. Magic coursed through him. He tried to let go, but his hands, or whatever he was using to hold on to the power, refused to respond. His vision went red, all except for a vein of gold that seemed to split the world.

"Radek."

With that word, the pain receded. The vein of gold pulsed, and though he couldn't see her, he had the definite impression that Rania was there.

"Radek. Calm yourself."

"What's happening?"

"You have touched the remnants of dead dragons. Your mind is not prepared to deal with beings like that."

"What do I do?"

"Find my mind. Reach out to it and follow it back. They will stop you if they can."

Radek nodded, or whatever passed for nodding in this strange mindscape, and opened his thoughts, searching for Rania. The chilling power of dragon spirits surrounded him. They seemed to be almost shapeless blobs of power. He could sense the anger within them. They lashed out at him, but he managed to stay just out of reach as he continued to search. He found Rania exactly where he expected to, right in the middle of the vein of gold.

Her mind was like a bright reflection of the others around him, stronger than some but weaker than most. Still, there was something about her that held the others back. There was a stability to her that felt vaguely familiar, and it took him a second to recognize it as dragon magic. He allowed himself to sink into it and sensed a line of energy stretching away from them. He thought he could see how it was done, and he had the sense that it was only because Rania was allowing him to see it. He lacked the strength to duplicate it. Instead, he grabbed on to her power, and the next thing he knew, he was back in his own body, gasping. Rania stood over him with a hand on his chest. Lines of gold glowed across her skin, but they faded when she saw he was awake.

"That was aptly done. I expected to have to assist you more than I did."

"If you two are done," Brenna said, "maybe we can figure out what to do about this graveyard."

"Yes, of course. Their spirits must be restless indeed to affect Radek as they did. I suspect the goblins are using that power to help build their dreadnaughts." She stepped forward. "Come, it is this way."

She led them through a series of forks. Radek was still disoriented from his experiences and had trouble walking for a few minutes. Once, he slipped on a patch of mud and cut a gash down his arm. He waved away his friends' concern, and they continued on.

After half an hour, they saw light ahead. He almost ran to it but hesitated at a look from Rania. She mumbled under her breath, and as they stepped out, they found themselves on the same ledge they had entered from. *Wind* sat a little ways away, exactly the way they had left her.

"Rania," Radek said.

The dragon shook her head. "It appears that a distracting spell has been placed on the cavern. It must be a subtle one for me not to detect it."

"Can you get around it?"

"Now that I know what to look for, I believe so."

They went back into the cave, but after half an hour, they found themselves exiting again. Rania scowled.

"What's going on?" Brenna asked. "Can't you see through it?"

Rania huffed, and for a second, it seemed like smoke streamed out of her nostrils. "It is dragon magic. I am proficient, certainly, but my focus was always more on the technological than the mystical. This was crafted by a true dragon gold spinner." She turned to Radek. "I will require your aid."

"Me?" Radek asked. "If you can't get past it, what do you expect me to do?"

"It is the true strength of shapers. The magic of any one race has difficultly stopping them. With your help, we should be able to see through this."

Radek's' blood felt like it turned to ice, but he nodded. "What do I do?"

"Simply cast a standard spell to see through veils. I will feed you magic."

Radek stared at her. "I don't know how to do that."

She raised an eyebrow. "Haven't you spent time learning human magic? I do not believe that spell is overly complicated."

Radek winced. "Not really. I've been learning about the magic of other races. I haven't really looked at human magic, aside from my lessons with Stregoi."

"That's hardly what I meant." Rania sighed and turned to Ovian. "What of you? Do you know how to see past illusions?"

Ovian nodded. "It's not that hard."

"Good. Radek, I take it you can combine our powers."

Radek's face went red. "Yes, I know how to do that."

"Good. After you, Ovian."

Ovian bowed his head and started singing. Radek's vision sharpened, and his hearing grew more acute. He scowled at the taste of mold in the air, and the mixture of odors almost made him gag. He took a moment to brace himself before grabbing onto his friend's power. The now-familiar elven magic suffused him with warmth. On the other hand, Rania's magic felt like a blazing inferno, or at least it would have if such an inferno could be controlled so precisely. There was a similarity in the two powers, not in their nature but in their intended goal. That made it easier than almost any combination he had ever made. He focused on that similarity and used it to fuse the powers together. The magic turned and headed for his eyes, but at the last second, he redirected it toward Rania. She shimmered as Radek's senses returned to normal, and she beckoned for them to follow.

Once again, she led them into the cave, but this time, she went through smaller openings that Radek didn't even notice until she passed through them. Once, she even approached what appeared to be a solid stone wall, but she passed through it like it wasn't there. The three friends exchanged glances before following.

Gradually, the air grew hotter, and a sulfurous scent overtook the moldy smell. Ovian, who never liked being underground, had the hardest time of it. Since elves were closer to plants than animals, he was especially sensitive to changes in the air. He pulled a small crystal out of his belt pouch and sang under his breath. The power flowing from Ovian to Radek quivered as the elf sang a second spell, but Ovian, apparently, had no trouble separating the two, and the magics never mixed. After a second, he took a deep breath as his crystal began to glow. He took a deep breath and smiled. Radek guessed it was the same spell his friend had so often used when they were in space in order to maintain the air.

Suddenly, Rania lifted a hand. "Hold."

"What is it?" Brenna asked.

"There is a web of power ahead of us, different from the distractor spell. It appears to be dragon magic mixed with goblin and dwarven. A touch of human as well."

"A trap?" Ovian asked.

"So it would seem. Radek, can you see it?"

Radek concentrated but shook his head. "I would have to let go of the spell seeing through the illusions."

"Do it," Rania said. "It will be easy enough to restart should we need it."

Radek nodded and let the power go. He concentrated on the area ahead of them. The human power was the easiest to detect, though Rania was right. There was only a bit of it. It shone like dozens of specks of light. As he focused, he saw a glowing cloud appear around the specks. Cold goblin power mixed with the pulsing power of the dwarves and with the warmth of the dragons; it filled the entire passage before them.

"I see it. I'm not sure what it does, but I don't think we can get past it without activating it."

"Goblin traps are usually quite deadly," Rania said. "They are normally brittle too, but the shaper's work may have remedied that. You three should retreat to around the last bend. I will attempt to disarm it, though I may set it off if I fail."

"Won't that hurt you?"

Rania laughed and motioned down to her body. "Do not mistake my appearance. I am still every bit as resilient as I am in my natural form." She waved at the passage before them. "Whatever that spell does, I can sense that there is not enough power in it to do me any lasting harm. Now go. I will be fine."

The trio nodded and retreated. Radek closed his eyes and concentrated. He could feel Rania's power swell within her. The dragon shaped the power into half a dozen strands of energy, each as sharp as a razor. They lashed forward, cutting into the glowing cloud, which parted as if it were a solid object that been sliced open. Smoke spilled out, and Rania let out a puzzled sound.

"Well, that was unexpected."

"What? "Brenna asked. "Are we safe?"

"Safe?" Rania asked. "No, I very much doubt it. It wasn't a trap, however."

"It wasn't?" Radek asked as he came around the corner.

Rania was examining the remnants of the spell. Bands of power seemed to writhe from the walls, and Radek realized what she had seen before she said it.

"It was an alarm. I believe we will be attacked soon."

As if on cue, a roar sounded through the cave, and the ground shook as something huge approached.

CHAPTER 22

P repare yourselves for battle," Rania said.

"Battle?" Brenna asked. "We haven't really done that."

Ovian, however, had already pulled a handful of crystals from his pouch and sang enchantments into them. He handed each of them two crystals.

"Speed, healing, warmth, and air. Without knowing what we're about to fight, it's the best I can do."

Radek nodded and took a deep breath, glad for the spell that provided him with air instead of having to breathe the sulfurous atmosphere of the cave. Brenna was obviously worried as she held hers up, though Radek knew her concern had nothing to do with magic. The three of them had been in plenty of battles before. Of course, most of those had been in *Wind*. Most, but not all.

"Don't worry," Radek said. "It'll be just like when we attacked the control room of the ring ship."

"You do remember almost dying when we did that, right?"

Ovian looked to the ceiling. "You act like we don't almost die all the time."

Brenna glared at him, though the banter had obviously calmed her down a little. She gripped her rune necklace in the same hand as the crystals, and Radek felt a surge of power. He closed his eyes and tried to sense whatever was coming, but the magic coming from his friends hung over them like a fog, blocking his senses. He sighed and released his grip on his power.

The heavy footsteps drew near, and they all prepared to attack, though Radek wasn't sure what he could actually do. There was movement in the shadows just beyond the reach of Rania's light. Radek could just make out the vague silhouette of a goblin. Brenna lifted a blaster and fired, though the goblin didn't react. Radek raised an eyebrow at the weapon.

"What?" she asked without looking at him. "After everything we've been through, are you surprised?"

The goblin stepped forward, its footsteps like thunder. Radek gasped as he saw that it was made of stone and stood at least two feet taller than any goblin he had ever seen. Brenna's shot had barely scorched the stone. It held a sword in its right hand and an ax in its left. Its eyes glowed bright red. This wasn't a goblin. This was a golem. Before any of them could say anything, it leaped.

Its stone sword moved faster than Radek's eyes could follow, even with Ovian's speed enchantment. The blade slammed into Rania's neck. Had it been anyone else, Radek was sure the blow would have decapitated them. Rania, however, barely winced. She hit the golem with a backhanded blow. There was no way flesh hitting stone should have done anything but hurt the flesh. Instead, the golem reeled back, and a chip of stone flew off of its face. It didn't even hesitate before attacking again. This time, Radek felt a surge of all four magics within it. A sickly green light surrounded the ax as it struck Rania's side. This time, the weapon cut through her dress and left a line of glowing blood.

Radek could only stare at the wound, but Ovian jumped at the golem, singing a high-pitched song. The elf specialized in wind magic, and he had always struggled in affecting earth, but still, the golem's skin rippled. Ovian shoved a crystal into its head and jumped off with a grace that made a cat seem clumsy. He landed behind the construct. He then looked at Radek.

"Go! Do it!"

"Do what?"

"Explode its head like last time!"

Brenna gaped at the elf before looking to Radek. "When did you explode a golem's head?"

The stone goblin slashed at Ovian, and the elf barely succeeded in rolling under it. Though the golem caught him in a hard kick that sent him across the cave floor. Radek hesitated for only a second before rushing forward. The golem had been distracted by Rania and Ovian and didn't notice him until he had wrapped his arms around its neck. It thrashed, but he held tight. The crystal Ovian had put in it was nothing special, just a simple warmth crystal, but that wasn't why Ovian had done it. Radek reached into the magic and pulled it out, even as he seized the power animating the statue. The four magics swirled within it, enabling it to be stronger than a golem created by any one race's magic. To create a construct like this required an expert hand and a delicate balancing of magic. What Radek did was not delicate. Destruction never was.

Radek tugged harder on the power in the crystal and forced it together with the magic animating the golem. The powers intermingled with each other, but rather than become unstable like most of the other times he had mixed magics, the power in the golem shuddered. Then the elven magic was expelled with such force that it actually threw Radek free. His head slammed against a rock, and the world spun. His skin tingled from the touch of the magic, and for a moment, he wasn't sure where he was. Strong hands gripped him, and he blinked to see Brenna at his side. He looked up at the golem, which was fully engaged in fighting Rania and Ovian, though the elf seemed to be limping slightly. A chunk was missing from the golem's head, and Radek could see a clump of bones.

"What happened?" Brenna asked.

"I think they were ready for me." He pointed at the bones and could almost see the power flowing through them. "Shoot that."

She stared at him for a moment before nodding and pointed her blaster. She aimed for a moment before firing. The blast hit the stone at the base of its neck. She said something under her breath and fired again. This time, it hit the bones as the golem slashed at Rania. The stone goblin grew sluggish. Rania slid around it and brought her hand down on the exposed bone. She grabbed it and pulled. The bone crackled, and shards flew free. The golem shuddered before falling to the ground. The light in its eyes faded. It squealed once and then went silent.

Ovian stood up and dusted himself off. He took a few steps. He was still limping, though not as much. Apparently, he had gotten better at crafting healing crystals. He looked from Radek to Rania and then to the downed golem. Then, he smiled.

"That went well. Should we keep going?"

CHAPTER 23

Radek had a bump on his head that pulsed with pain, and when he brought his fingers to it, they came away bloody. After a few seconds, however, it became more bearable. Ovian's healing crystal would take care of it before too long. He felt a little nauseous as he combined Ovian's and Rania's magic again, but he managed to hold onto it. They progressed more slowly than before. They came upon other alarm spells, but now that they knew what they were, Rania was able to disable them without any trouble. After about a quarter-hour, they came to a four-way fork. Rania looked down one and then another. She pointed down one.

"The graveyard is that way."

"Let's go, then," Radek said. "Maybe we can stop them from using dragon magic at all."

"No," Rania said. "There is something more pressing down this way."

She didn't wait for them to respond before heading into the cave she had indicated. Radek and the others followed, but it wasn't long before the dragon started running, going much faster than anyone on two legs should have been able to. In a few seconds, they had lost her. Fortunately, the cave didn't fork again, and after a few minutes, they came to a wide chamber that glowed with an eerie orange light. Dozens of spheres, each bigger than Radek himself, littered the floor. Radek had seen a chamber like this on the merfolk homeworld. There, the goblins had captured sea serpent eggs in order to tap into their innate magic. If the horrified look on Rania's face was any indication, these had not been laid by the great serpents.

"Dragon eggs." The air around her glowed with power, so much that Radek had to back away to avoid being burned. Even the ground rippled in response to her anger. "These goblin beasts have dragon eggs."

"Where did they even get them?" Radek asked.

"I have no idea." Rania spoke through clenched teeth, "but this can't be allowed. I need to take them out of here as soon as possible."

"What about the graveyard?"

She waved her hand, and the eggs, all of them, lifted into the air. "You know where it is."

Brenna pulled out her pocket computer and nodded. "I have our coordinates, and I can detect another chamber nearby."

Rania nodded. "That is it. Deliver those coordinates to your people and have them destroy it the same way you did the shipyard. I will take care of these."

She didn't wait for them to respond. She threw back her head and roared. It shook the chamber, and Radek's flesh felt like it would turn to jelly. A stream of fire shot out of Rania's mouth, crashing against the stone ceiling. It glowed a brilliant red, and after a few seconds, molten rock dripped onto the ground. The heat was becoming too much, and Radek and his friends backed up until they were against a wall.

Red light flooded the room, and the air rippled in the heat. Radek tried to see what was going on, but the stone glowed too brightly. He squinted and caught a glimpse of Rania, now back in her true form, albeit smaller, still spewing fire at the ceiling. The dragon roared, and the ceiling collapsed, letting in the sunlight. There was a woosh as the heat inside the cavern met the cold air outside. Then, Rania flew out so fast that the air from her wings pressed Radek and his friends against the wall.

For several seconds, the three friends could only stare at each other. Brenna spoke first.

"Well, that was unexpected."

"Yeah," Radek said. "Can you call *Wind* from here?"

Brenna tapped her pocket computer, which had a longer range than their mystical connection. "Yes." She waved at the newly opened cavern ceiling. "That opening lets the signal get through. She's on her way."

Less than a minute later, *Wind* flew into the cavern. The floor was uneven, but she managed to place herself so that she was stable until the three of them got in. Then, she hovered a few inches off the ground while they got situated.

"Did you see Rania leave?" Radek asked.

"Indeed. She had surrounded herself in a carrier spell. She had what appeared to be dragon eggs. I couldn't tell where she was heading, but it definitely wasn't for the fleet."

Radek bit his lower lip and nodded. "She probably doesn't want to trust anyone else with those eggs."

"We found them," Ovian said with a wide grin.

"Rania found them," Brenna said.

"I helped," Ovian said. "Radek was using my spell, too."

"Forget about it." Brenna tapped her pocket computer. "*Wind*, can you transmit these coordinates to the rest of the fleet? They need to be bombed."

"They *need* to be reduced to a pool of molten earth," Ovian said, "and then bombed. Twice."

Wind beeped, and the avatar bowed its head. "General Verren acknowledged and will consider your request."

Radek rolled his eyes. "Tell him it's a dragon graveyard and that the goblins are using that to power their strongest spells, including the ones that were probably used to build the nova dragons."

Wind beeped again and responded almost immediately. "He will redirect the attacking fleet."

"Good," Radek said. "We'll join them." He reached for the control sphere but hesitated. "Go ahead, Brenna."

He could imagine her smile as the ship lifted off. He tapped the sensors and found the attacking fleet heading toward them. The coordinates of the graveyard weren't far. They would be able to hit it as soon as they gained more altitude.

The blast hit them without warning. A beam of green energy shot out from a hole in the ground. *Wind*'s shields glowed so brightly; they became almost solid. The ship jerked to one side as Brenna tried to get out of the beam's way, but it stayed locked on.

"*Wind*," she called out. "Full speed. Divert any power you can to the engines."

Radek was pressed back into his seat as the starfighter accelerated to a speed that even overwhelmed the inertial dampeners. A heartbeat later, however, *Wind* shook violently, and they began losing altitude.

"What's happening?" Radek asked.

"The goblin weapon pierced my shields."

"They've never had anything that could do that so fast."

"It appears they were tapping into much of the power generated by the graveyard. The amount of power was incalculable."

"How much longer until we hit the ground?"

Wind didn't have a chance to answer before they slammed into the ground so hard that half the ship was driven into the earth.

CHAPTER 24

Is everyone okay?" Radek asked. It hurt to speak, and he tasted blood. He brought a hand to his lips, and his fingers came away red.

"I think so," Brenna said.

Ovian put his hand to his forehead and took a deep breath. After a few seconds, he looked up and nodded. "I'm fine."

The front window had shattered. The entire front of the ship was underground, and dirt and rocks had come into the cockpit. Tall trees rose up around them, though there were no animal sounds. Any creatures had probably been scared away by the crash.

"*Wind*, status?"

The avatar appeared on the screen, though it spoke as if through static, and the image flickered. "Shields are completely inoperable. Hull is severely damaged. Weapons are inoperable. Communications are inoperable. Engines are inoperable. Gold drive is inoperable."

"Self-repair?"

"Severely damaged. That system can repair itself. Once that is done, it can address the other systems."

"How long will that take?"

"Eight days."

"That's too long," Brenna said. "The goblins know they shot us down. They'll be looking for us. They'll want to salvage anything they can from *Wind* if nothing else."

"Can you focus on the engines?" Radek asked. "Maybe if we can repair those, we can get back to the *Linala*."

The avatar shook her head, and the screen fuzzed. For a second, it looked like she wouldn't come back. She eventually reappeared, though it was only as a vague outline. "The self-repair system must repair itself before it can fix anything else. That will take at least a day."

"That means no communications either," Brenna said. She took a deep breath. "Self-destruct?"

"What?" Radek and Ovian spoke at once. They exchanged glances before Radek went on. "We can't destroy *Wind*."

"Radek, she has advanced technology, and her memory core contains enough intelligence on the Vanelian fleet to make sure the goblins win."

"But…" Ovian sputtered. "She's the most advanced ship in the galaxy."

Brenna raised an eyebrow. "And do you want her to fall into goblin hands? She's the main reason they'd come looking for us."

"Well…no."

"She's just a machine," Brenna said. "Rania can build another one."

Radek thought he saw tears in Ovian's eyes. "*Wind* is our friend."

"*Wind*, is your core personality module damaged?"

Once again, the screen fuzzed. "It does not appear so, though some of the links to it have been damaged."

"Core what?" Ovian asked.

Brenna ignored him. "Can you remove it?"

"I can, though if I do, I will no longer be able to control any systems."

Brenna turned to the other two. "There you go."

Radek blinked. "What do you mean? What were you talking about?"

She let out a breath and rolled her eyes. "I know you have a gift for magic, but we have talked about how *Wind* is the most advanced ship in the galaxy. Maybe you should spend at least some time learning about her technological side. All we need to do is get *Wind* to start the self-destruct timer. Then, we extract the core personality module and take it with us. Rania can put it in some other ship she builds."

"I don't understand," Radek said. "What is a core personality module?"

"It's *Wind,*" Brenna said. "Her personality. Her memories. Everything that makes her *her*. Rania can put it in another ship, and in every important way, it will be her."

"I will miss being this ship," *Wind* said. "Brenna is right, however. I cannot guarantee repairs will be completed before I am captured, and I have no wish to be captured by the goblins. I believe arming the self-destruct would be our best option."

"How long will we have once you start the timer before detonation?"

"It can be set for anywhere between a few minutes to several hours."

"We don't really need hours," Radek looked to Brenna and Ovian. "How long?"

Ovian just shook his head but didn't say anything. Brenna pursed her lips and pulled out her pocket computer. She tapped it a few times before sighing.

"It's hard to say. I'm not sure where we are. We were going pretty fast when we got shot down, so I don't have a map of this area. From what I saw, the forest is pretty thick around here, and I don't know how fast we can move through it."

"We'll just have to risk it. Is there anything else we need from the ship?"

They did a quick search and found a few ration tablets. *Wind*'s self-repair systems worked on a molecular level, and as such, they could synthesize a variety of items. The ration tablets she produced could sustain them for several days but tasted only slightly better than dirt. Radek sighed and slipped them into his pockets. He looked at Brenna.

"Five minutes?"

The dwarf let out a long breath. "It will have to be good enough. *Wind*, do your sensors work well enough to give me some idea of where you are?"

"Negative," *Wind* said. "Sensor and navigation data is inaccessible."

"So much for that idea." She took a deep breath. "*Wind*, set a self-destruct timer for five minutes and eject your core personality module."

"That command requires the approval of both of the primary users."

Radek's mouth felt dry. Rania had originally gifted *Wind* to him and Ovian before they even knew Brenna. They had granted her access to *Wind*'s systems, but there were apparently some commands that still required the two of them. Radek swallowed and nodded.

"Do it."

"Ovian, do you agree?" *Wind* asked.

For a moment, Ovian froze. Radek could practically see the thoughts on his friend's face. He was the one who had given the self-destruct command to the space station *Vanel*. Now, he had to do the same thing again, only he had to give the command to an entity he cared about. Radek walked up next to his friend and put a hand on his shoulder.

"We're taking *Wind* with us," he said. "There's no reason not to do this."

Ovian bit his lower lip and nodded. "I know. *Wind*, do as they say."

"Self-destruct command acknowledged." The screen went dark. Radek felt a surge of magic as a metal box was ejected from beneath the main display. Radek took it and handed it to Brenna.

"We should get going quickly," she said as she tucked it away. "It's going to be a pretty big explosion."

Radek nodded. He took a quick look around. Off to the east, the forest got thicker, and the land sloped downward. From what he had seen of goblin bases, they tended to build them in the open, so that was probably the safest way to go. He motioned for the others to follow and headed in that direction. They hadn't been moving very long when a brilliant fireball erupted behind them. The ground shook, and even at their distance, a wave of heat washed over them. Dirt and rocks flew into the air, and Radek coughed as a cloud of dust rolled over them. He wrinkled his nose at the smell of burning wood and panicked for a moment.

"Did we just start a forest fire?"

Ovian shook his head. "Goalton trees have a higher water content than most."

Radek calmed down but looked toward the explosion. "Did either of you know it would be that big?"

Ovian shook his head, but Brenna just kept staring at the column of smoke that rose from the remnants of what had once been the *Stellar Wind*. Finally, she shook her head as well.

"No, but it makes sense. We still had some stellar core missiles. Those were probably detonated too. Come on, the goblins won't have missed that, and I'd rather be out of here before they send out search parties."

Radek threw one last glance and the site of the explosion before heading deeper into the forest.

CHAPTER 25

They didn't see signs of anyone searching until they had been walking for over an hour. A goblin ship flew over them, so low that they smelled its exhaust. It broke off some of the highest branches. Ovian winced at that, but they kept going. According to the elf, something in the trees' composition interfered with scanners, which was the only reason they hadn't been detected yet. Brenna took the lead through the forest, periodically looking down at her pocket computer.

"I thought that thing needed *Wind*'s sensors to tell you where we are," Radek said.

"It does," Brenna said as she tapped her screen, "or at least it does to do it accurately. *Wind* got some readings of the land before we crashed. We were going too fast for it to be entirely accurate, but it gives me an idea, at least."

"Where are we?"

"About thirty miles from the graveyard," she said. "Maybe forty."

"That's not very specific."

"It's the best I can do," Brenna said.

"Good enough," Ovian said. "Let's go."

Radek and Brenna both looked at him. "To the graveyard?"

"Yes."

"Why would we go there?"

"Because it's about to be attacked."

They both stared at him, but he gave no other explanation. Finally, Radek rolled his eyes.

"Again, why would we go there?"

Ovian looked up to the sky. "Well, the reason we don't signal the fleet from Brenna's computer is that the goblins will detect the signal and be able to find us, right?"

Brenna nodded. "Yes, but I'm a little surprised you realized that."

Ovian let out a breath. "Just because technology doesn't usually make sense doesn't mean I don't understand it at all. Anyway, there will already be a lot of goblin ships at the graveyard, but they'll be distracted. If we can signal the attacking fleet, they might be able to pick us up before the goblins can do anything about it."

Radek and Brenna exchanged glances before Brenna spoke. "That's actually a good idea, Ovian. We have to get there quickly, though. The fleet will already be on their way."

"Can you detect them?" Radek asked.

Brenna tapped her screen and shook her head. "They want the attack to be a surprise, so they'll probably come into the atmosphere right on top of it." She sighed. "There's no way we can cover thirty miles before the attack is over."

"But they will be scanning the area after the attack is done to make sure they got everything," Radek said. "It's still our best chance."

Another ship passed over them. This time, the passing made a large branch break off, and they had to scramble to avoid being hit by the falling debris. It clipped Radek, and he tumbled to the ground. At first, he thought his arm had been cut, but when he touched it, his fingers came away sticky with tree sap instead of blood. They all laughed at that, and they had just started up again when something howled behind them. A chill ran down Radek's spine. He had heard about this.

"Wargs?"

Ovian nodded. "I think so. I've heard they're too much trouble to transport enough of them off-world to make it worth it, but on Goalton, they use them for hunting all the time."

"They'll find us," Brenna said. She eyed Ovian. "Can you do anything to mask our scent from giant wolves?"

"No," Ovian said, but then his face brightened. "Actually, yes."

He lifted his arms and sang. A gentle breeze stirred, so mild that Radek would have thought it was natural if he didn't know better. It swirled around them before dying down.

"What was that?"

"I can't really stop them from smelling us," Ovian said. "Their noses are too good, but I did carry our smell all over the place."

Radek grinned. "So they'll know we're out here."

Ovian smiled as wide as Radek had ever seen. "Which they already do, but they won't have any idea where we are because they'll smell us everywhere."

Another howl pierced the night. This one was closer, and all three of their smiles vanished. Brenna spoke in a low whisper. "Maybe we should be quiet anyway."

Radek nodded, and once again, the dwarf took the lead. Several times, they heard ships nearby. Once, there was a low rumbling that Brenna swore was a dwarven vessel, but her pocket computer couldn't detect any identifier, so it was impossible to tell if it came from the Vanelian fleet or if it was one of the Necal. By silent agreement, they didn't contact it.

As the hours ticked by, the patrols became more and more numerous. All the time they spent hiding reduced their progress to a crawl.

"We'll never get there like this," Ovian said after they'd been crouching under a bush for nearly an hour.

"Do you have a better idea?" Radek asked, trying to ignore his aching muscles from being in the same position for so long. Ovian gave him a smile that made Radek's blood turn to ice. "Why do I get the feeling I'm about to regret asking that?"

Brenna shrugged. "Because you're reasonably intelligent for a human."

"We should steal some wargs," Ovian said.

Both Brenna and Radek stared at him. "You can't be serious."

"What?" Ovian asked. "They can run really fast."

"How exactly do you propose we catch a giant wolf trained by goblins to rip our throats out if they catch us?" Brenna asked.

"Radek can do it."

Radek blinked. "I can?"

"You've done all that work with mental magic," Ovian said. "You can just take control of them."

"If by 'all that work' you mean that I had one fight with Derek, and Rania had to help me."

"Right," Ovian said. "Do what you did then."

"I don't think it works like that."

Ovian looked at the sky. "Between the two of us, who has the better idea of how magic works?"

Radek opened his mouth to respond but closed it again. Ovian did have a point there, though as far as Radek knew, the elf had never studied mental magic. Brenna sighed.

"I know I should argue with you, but I recognize that look on your face. It wouldn't do any good, would it?"

"None whatsoever," Ovian said. "Go ahead, Radek."

Radek looked from one to another before letting out a long breath. He closed his eyes and concentrated, reaching out, though not quite knowing what he was looking for. There were a pair of powerful minds near him. He reached out and touched one.

It was like diving into a river of song. The music reached out, touching everything. He felt like he was flying. The wind surrounded him. Then, the air shifted, catching him up in it. It carried him out of the river, and the next thing he knew, he was back in his body, on the ground. Ovian stood over him.

"Why did you do that?"

"Do what?"

"You tried to get into my mind."

"I did?"

The elf nodded. "It's a good thing I recognized you. I almost attacked before I did."

Radek sat up and took several deep breaths and turned to Brenna. "I sensed you too. I think this might actually work if I can find the right mind. Hold on."

He closed his eyes again. Now that he had a better idea of what he was looking at, he could see that Ovian's was more ethereal with a shape that constantly shifted. Brenna was more solid, and there was an almost machine-like quality to her, to the point where he even thought he smelled oil. Radek extended his senses farther. After a few minutes, he sensed something, but he couldn't be sure if it was goblin or warg. Tentatively, he reached forward. A chill washed over him. He pulled back for a second but gritted his teeth and pushed forward. Red surrounded him. He could see the world, but that almost didn't matter. Sight was dull and practically useless. Smell, on the other hand…he could smell *everything*.

A deer a quarter-mile away sensed the coming of his pack and darted away. They could chase it down if they wanted to, but they had been given other commands by the pack leader. Something prickled in the back of his mind. He didn't want to follow those orders. There was something else. Something that mattered more. He slowed, allowing the pack to pull away from him. One of them barked at him, demanding that he keep up and follow the directions given to them by the goblins. That was it. Just one bark, and it was all he could do to resist the command. Had the other stopped and tried to impose its will on Radek, he wasn't sure he could have resisted, but though he had been able to shake off the goblins' command, they still held the minds of the others, and they kept running.

Radek pulled away and sniffed at the air. He found the scent he was looking for, but there was too much of it. He thought that made sense, though. He couldn't remember why. Even so, he knew which way he should go and took off in that direction. He ran so fast his legs scarcely seemed to touch the ground. The forest passed in a blur, and the next thing he knew, he stood before three beings. One had his eyes closed, and the other two got between him and it. Their scent brought a surge of excitement. These were the prey. He bared his teeth and growled, glad that he would be the one to take these people down.

CHAPTER 26

Radek," one of the beings said. "Is that you?"

The name rang in his mind. He knew it, but these were prey. It didn't matter what they said. He took a step forward. Two of them backed up, but they kept themselves between him and the last. That one just stood there with his eyes closed. The sight of that sent a chill racing through him. Abruptly, Radek's mind rushed forward, pushing back the warg's thoughts. He lay down. It was difficult to control both his own body and the warg, but he managed to walk over to the creature and get on. He spoke in an emotionless voice.

"Get on. I can't control more than one."

Ovian approached, and the warg's mind tried to break free, but Radek managed to hold on. The elf reached out and ran his fingers through the warg's fur. It tried to snap, but Radek held it back. When Ovian got on behind Radek, however, a low rumble shook the great wolf's body. Radek felt Ovian tense, but his friend didn't say anything. Brenna glared at them but followed a second later. Dwarves having unusually dense bones, she weighed more than the other two put together. He felt the wolf squirming in his mind, but Radek had managed to get a good grip on it. It wouldn't be able to break free. At least, he hoped it wouldn't.

"Don't let me fall off," he said before directing the wolf to run.

It had been amazing to run as the warg, to feel himself running through the land. Not only did he feel that now, he felt himself riding a warg through the forest at a speed that was almost unimaginable without a vehicle. He was the wind. He was speed itself.

All too soon, they had come out of the forest and overlooked the large field with the hole they had come out of in the center. Goblin ships filled the skies, and the grounds were littered with goblins and dwarves. A chill ran through Radek, one that had nothing to do with the temperature. The warg growled.

"Get off," he said.

"What?"

"Get off. I'm about to lose control."

Ovian and Brenna scrambled off. Radek tried to follow, but he couldn't move and control the creature at the same time. He was about to call for help, but he wasn't sure he could do even that. As the wolf, he sat on his haunches and felt the human body slide off. He hesitated for a second. The human was helpless, and nothing stoked his hunger more than helpless prey. He reached into himself for one last surge of strength before sending the creature running into the woods. In the next instant, he was back in his body with Brenna and Ovian standing over him.

"What did you do to it?" Brenna asked.

"I sent it into the woods."

"Won't it come after us?" Ovian asked. "Or report us or something?"

"I wiped its memory."

"I didn't know you could do that."

Radek sat up and let out a breath. "It's kind of like what I did to Derek. I'm pretty sure animals are easier than people, though. Don't worry about it."

"Pretty sure?" Brenna asked. "So it might be coming after us right now."

The hairs on the back of Radek's neck stood on end. "Maybe, but I don't think so. Look, with a little luck, we'll be gone in a few minutes anyway."

Another chill ran through him, and he looked toward the valley. Now that he wasn't focused on controlling the warg, he recognized it. Goblin magic. A lot of it.

"They're ready for an attack," Radek said. "They have their bone mages down here. They set a trap."

"Well, stop them," Ovian said.

"What do you expect me to do?"

"Disrupt their magic."

"I thought you knew more about magic than technology," Radek said. "I can't just disrupt a working that big."

Ovian looked at the sky. "Don't you know anything?"

Radek and Brenna exchanged glances. "Apparently not," Radek said.

"If there are that many bone mages working on something, you don't have to oppose all of them. You just have to find the linchpin. If you disrupt that one, the whole thing will collapse in on itself."

"How do I find the linchpin?"

Ovian stared into his eyes for several seconds. "I have no idea with goblins. I mean, I know the theory, but you're the only one who's actually *done* bone magic. Just look for something that looks linchpinny."

"That's not a real word," Radek said.

"Did you understand what I meant?"

"I guess so."

"Then it's enough of a word for me." Ovian grinned. "Come on. You don't want them to destroy the fleet, do you?"

Radek glared at him before closing his eyes. He reached for the cold power of the goblin's magic. He felt like he had reached into a wave of ice. The cold spread throughout his body, and for a moment, he thought he would freeze. He tried to find any sort of weakness, but it was the same thing as far as he could see. Finally, he pulled back. When he opened his eyes, the world was spinning, and it took him a few seconds to stop shivering. He managed to keep his balance and shook his head.

"Nothing linchpinny. Let me try again."

Ovian nodded, though Brenna looked uncertain. He tried to give her a reassuring smile, but given that he almost fell over as he did, he didn't think he was very successful. He had to do something, though, so he closed his eyes again. This time, he was better prepared. He clenched his teeth and tried to seize the spell, but it slipped through his fingers.

"That's weird," he said.

"What?" Ovian asked.

"It's all goblin magic, but I haven't seen a bone spell built like this. It flows more like dragon magic."

"Can you disrupt it? You're good at breaking stuff."

If Radek could have spared the concentration, he would have scowled. "I don't know. Give me a second."

As much as Radek hated to admit it, Ovian was right. Radek did have a tendency to wreck complex magical workings. The magics of different races were unstable if not combined exactly right, and it took a great deal of skill to do that. Breaking it was another thing entirely.

He reached inside himself, looking for the well of power that allowed him to sense the magic of others. He had only a vague understanding of his own magic. That had been increased by his training with Stregoi, and it was enough for him to do what he needed. He shoved his power into the goblin spell and waited, expecting it to collapse in on itself.

It didn't.

Radek tried again, but nothing happened. He pushed his magic into it a third time, but this time, he focused it. He felt the pieces of his power flowing through the spell, though they were slowly fading, their energy sucked up by a subtler working that he hadn't noticed before. The larger spell continued whatever it was doing as if Radek wasn't even there. He pulled back and sighed.

"I can't stop it. Whatever they're doing, they've protected themselves against me."

"How?"

Radek gave him a level look. "We weren't exactly sneaky when we got here, so they probably know we're on the planet. I don't think they noticed me, though. It looked more like an automated defense than something they were actively doing to counter me."

"Could you tell what they're doing?"

"No, but I wasn't really looking. Let me see if I can find out."

He closed his eyes again and reached out, but he found a cold that had nothing to do with goblin magic. It felt familiar, and it took him a few seconds to recognize it.

Death.

"I think I was wrong about them not noticing me."

"Why do you say that?" Ovian asked.

"There's death magic on the way. A lot of it."

"Necromancers?"

"I don't think so. It feels more like golems, only not exactly."

"How can something be not exactly golems?" Brenna asked.

Ovian looked up and was about to answer when he pointed and staired. Radek looked where he was pointing. It took him a few seconds to see what his friend meant. It was hard to see the white against the blue of the sky.

"Ghosts."

CHAPTER 27

Before long, there were so many ghosts in the sky that they looked like stars, in spite of it being day. Apparently, the spirits didn't know where Radek and his friends were because they fanned out as they dove to the ground. Radek, Ovian, and Brenna hid in some bushes, though Radek wasn't entirely sure that would do any good. He was relatively certain ghosts used a form of magic to see, so he didn't think the bushes would hide them. Still, the three of them didn't say anything for a long time. Once, a ghost hovered over them for several minutes before floating away. Radek reached out with his mind and tentatively tried to touch one of the spirits.

Something screamed in his mind, and he felt like there were chains of solid ice wrapped around him, pulling him along. It was like when he had taken control of the warg, only this time, it was the other way around. Some powerful force dragged both him and the spirit along. He was ready to attack the invaders to this world, though it was completely against his will. The ghost didn't want to either. He tried to pull back, but the chains held him just as tightly as they did the ghost.

"Radek?"

The voice seemed to come from far away. He knew it had to come from his friends, but he couldn't tell if it was Ovian or Brenna. He tried to answer them, but the restraints stopped him from speaking. He couldn't escape. That only left one option. He drew on his own power, of human magic, and threw it against the chains. His power crashed against it like waves on the shore. He tried again, but he may as well be trying to wash away a mountain. The chains were just too strong.

"Radek?"

The voice came again. Someone started singing, and it took him longer than it should have to realize it was Ovian. The elven magic wrapped around him, contrasting with the cold of the chains. Radek grabbed to it, mingling it with his own power. That made it stronger, though not strong enough. He still couldn't break the chains, but he managed to move them. The ghost screamed and tried to get away, but the chains were specifically designed to hold beings such as it. Radek was another matter. He slipped out of the bonds. The next thing he knew, he was on the ground gasping, with his friends standing over him. Again.

"What happened?" Ovian asked.

"I didn't realize it was that strong. I almost got lost." He waved at the sky. "The goblins took control of those ghosts, but they're not looking for us."

"Then, what are they doing?"

Thunder crashed, and the sky seemed to ignite as elven starships burst into the atmosphere. The ghosts swarmed, closing in on the invaders, and the fighters seemed to lose control. Some ran into each other while others plummeted to the ground. The earth and sky rumbled with explosions. Radek could feel magic in the air as the elves tried songs of their own to save themselves.

"They were getting ready to do that."

"Stop them," Ovian said. "You practiced death magic."

"I had one lesson. Can't you stop them?"

"Ghosts don't really care about wind."

A missile shot from one of the ships before it lost control. The projectile slammed into the ground and exploded, sending up a shower of molten earth and stone. Bone fragments rained from the sky. Brenna pulled out her pocket computer and tapped the screen.

"At least they got that much. They're attacking the graveyard. I'm trying to contact someone in the fleet."

"Won't the goblins find us?" Radek asked.

She waved at the sky without looking up. "With all of that going on, I doubt they'll notice one more transmission."

Goblin ships zipped across the sky to engage the Vanelian ships. With the attacking fleet already disoriented by the ghosts, the goblins ripped through them like they were toys piloted by children. Some of the dragon-built ships managed to hold their own, but the ghosts and goblins focused their attention on those, and before long, they too fell. Ovian lifted his hands and gathered power to himself.

"If we can't stop the ghosts, maybe we can help our side win the battle. Hold on."

Ovian sang loud and clear. The wind picked up, but this was nothing like Radek had ever seen his friend do. It howled, and trees bent before its fury. Small rocks stung, and they were driven at him by the wind. It almost carried him away, but Brenna latched one arm to him while holding on to a tree with another. Boulders were picked up and flew toward the goblin ships. Even with his command of the wind, Radek knew there was no way Ovian could actually aim those rocks, but there were so many goblin vessels that it didn't matter. Rocks and trees bounced against goblin shields. Most of the time, they were simply incinerated by the energy barrier, but every once in a while, a ship shook as its shields winked out. The elves were ready, in spite of their distraction, and made short work of them. Radek grabbed his friend.

"Come on."

"We have to help them."

Brenna grabbed his other hand. "Do you think the goblins will just not notice a major elf song being sung so close to their boneyard? They're probably on their way already."

"She's right," Radek said.

Ovian looked at the sky and sang a couple more notes before lowering his hands. He was breathing heavily, but he nodded and led them into the forest. They had gone at least a hundred yards before the elf stopped and looked at Brenna.

"Did you contact anyone?"

"I don't know. No one responded, but they were a little busy."

"That's why the ghosts were there," Radek said. "They were getting ready to attack. I don't think they detected me after all."

"Will you make up your mind?" Ovian said.

Radek glared at him. "It means they're not looking for us. If Brenna's message got through, then General Verren might send someone."

"So, we just wait here?" Ovian asked. "Shouldn't we at least do *something?*"

"Like what?" Radek asked.

"Here's an idea," Brenna said as she tapped her pocket computer. "Maybe we could rescue the prisoners."

"What?" Ovian and Radek said at the same time.

"I intercepted some of their communications. Some of the elves who were shot down when we attacked the shipyards survived." She gripped her computer tighter. "They're prisoners of the Necal."

"What? Where?"

"Half a mile south. They're being transported to a prisoner camp. I'm not sure why, but if we get to them before they get to their destination, we might be able to free them."

"If we do that, they'll definitely know we're here," Radek said.

"Are you saying we should leave them?" Ovian asked.

Radek was about to say no, but he didn't get a chance. The elf was already running to the south. Brenna sighed but took off after him. Radek followed on her heels.

CHAPTER 28

I f Radek hadn't spent so much time on Droshala, running through a forest would have been dangerous. With such uneven ground, it would be too easy to twist an ankle or worse, but his time on the elven homeworld had honed his reflexes, and he moved through it almost as quickly as he could have through flat land. Brenna was nearly as capable, but Ovian, who had the best reflexes of the three, pulled ahead until he was out of sight. Radek kept heading in the same general direction. He leaped over a low bush and crashed into Ovian, who had been squatting on the other side. They had just started to get up when Brenna rammed into them, bringing all three of them to the ground.

"Can't you two watch where you're going?" Ovian asked.

"Why did you stop?" Radek asked.

Ovian pointed. Radek could just see movement in the brush, and after a moment, he heard dwarven voices. He was hardly an expert in the dwarven language, but it seemed they hadn't noticed the three of them. The voices were yelling at someone. Ovian held up a hand and crept forward. Radek followed, moving as quietly as he could.

Four Necal in black armored battle suits were guiding at least two dozen elves and dwarves, as well as a pair of shapeshifters in half-wolf form. Brenna pulled out her blaster and pointed. Radek wished he had brought one as well. Instead, he focused, trying to gather power to himself. It slipped through his fingers a few times before he finally got a tentative grip. Ovian sung a soft song while holding a red crystal, which began glowing with a harsh green light. The wind around them shifted in response, and one of the elves looked in their direction. Radek recognized him as a singer who had a particular strength in earth magic. She looked right at where the three of them were hiding before shaking her head. Ovian didn't see, but Radek put a hand on Ovian's shoulder.

"No."

"What do you mean no? Do you realize who they have captured there? Two powerful singers and one of the best fighter pilots in the fleet."

"That earth singer…"

"Venulia," Brenna replied.

"Right. Singer Venulia doesn't want us to. I think she has a plan."

Ovian was about to argue but let out a breath and nodded. They followed the trapped pilots, keeping as close as they could without being seen. After a few hours, the sky began to darken, and heat seemed to drain out of the air. Ovian gave them each a warmth crystal. They weren't too powerful, as the elf was worried about being detected, but they served the keep the worst of the cold off of them. An hour after full dark had fallen, the Necal finally made camp, setting up canvas tents in a circle. The prisoners were chained to a nearby tree and left outside while the dwarves went inside.

"How far is this prisoner's camp anyway?" Radek asked.

Brenna shrugged. "I don't exactly have a map. I just know it was south. It can't be far, or they would have used vehicles."

Ovian shook his head. "Not in this forest. It doesn't like visitors."

"It's a forest, Ovian," Brenna said. "It's not conscious."

Ovian looked toward the sky. "All forests are conscious, this one more than most. The trees are speaking so loudly that it's hard to block them out. They wouldn't allow vehicles through it. Scanners wouldn't work very well either."

Brenna glared at him. "The forest is alive?"

"Obviously."

"Well, don't you think that would have been helpful to know before now?"

"Why? It's not like it would have made any difference. We still would have followed the prisoners."

"Yes, but we might have…We could have…" She threw her hands up in frustration.

"See," Ovian said. "It's not like you would have stopped checking your computer anyway."

Brenna gave him a level stare but didn't answer. Radek thought Ovian had a point but didn't say anything. They still hadn't had any sign from Venulia, and he was inclined to do something, regardless of what she said. He tried calling his power to himself, but when Ovian saw his expression, the elf shook his head.

"Military singers usually know what they're doing, and they get grumpy if you interfere with their plans. Let's give her one more day. If nothing happens by tomorrow night, we'll make our move."

Radek looked from the prisoners to Ovian and them to Brenna. The dwarf nodded, and Radek let out a sigh of resignation. They set up camp. Radek volunteered to take the first watch, as he didn't think he would be able to sleep, and they settled in for the night.

Radek stared at the camp for a few hours. Goalton had two moons, and both shone brightly, which was the only reason he was able to see the Necal camp. Dwarves having a much better night vision than humans, they had no fire. Only one of the Necal was awake, and he seemed to be entertaining himself by mocking one of the dwarven prisoners. With three of the four enemy soldiers asleep, Radek was confident they could have freed the prisoners. He might even be able to do it himself. He was tempted, in spite of what Ovian had said about the plans of elven singers. He had just about convinced himself to act when someone touched his shoulder. He jumped and turned, trying and failing to call up his magic. Brenna stood behind him, a wide grin on her face.

"My watch," she said. "Don't be so jumpy."

"Sorry." He looked around. "Given where we are…"

She nodded and glanced toward the camp. "I understand. Try to get some sleep."

He nodded and went to lay down near Ovian. The ground was soft, which seemed odd to him. For all the death and pain the goblins had caused in this war, it seemed unfair that the earth of their homeworld should be soft. He almost didn't want to sleep, as if by doing so, he would somehow spite the planet itself. Those thoughts didn't last long as he drifted to sleep.

The chains held him again, so cold they felt like they would freeze his blood. So many others were held prisoner. Some were so great that no magic should have been able to hold them, but yet it did. All around him, there were screams and roars of pain. It all pressed against his mind, squeezing him with the weight of a mountain, of an ocean. They would drive him insane with nothing more than their cries. It wasn't long before his voice had joined their screams.

"Be quiet," Ovian said.

Radek opened his eyes. The chains were gone, and the sky was lightening with the approach of dawn. He blinked away his sleep and sat up.

"What's going on?"

"You were screaming in your sleep," Ovian said. "Again."

"Wait," Brenna said. "The last time that happened, you had been possessed by an ancient sea god. Is that happening again?"

"We're not anywhere close to the sea," Ovian said.

She rolled her eyes. "You know what I mean. Is there some other super-powerful entity from the dawn of time that's decided possessing Radek is somehow the best way to achieve its goals?"

Ovian looked up. "What are the chances that would happen twice?"

"To us?" Brenna asked. "I'd say pretty high."

"I don't think that's what's happening," Radek said. "At least not on purpose. The goblins captured a lot of ghosts. I think I was just hearing them."

Brenna stared at him. "You were *just* hearing captured ghosts in your dreams, and they possessed you enough to make you scream in your sleep. You don't find this out of the ordinary?"

Radek sighed. "I probably should, but after everything that's happened, not really."

Brenna opened her mouth to speak but paused. After a second, she shrugged. "As much as I hate to admit it, you have a point there. Can you stop them from controlling you again?"

"I'm not sure. I don't think they were really controlling me. It's more like they were a current, and I was caught up in it. I'll just have to not go to sleep."

"Great," Ovian said. "That means we just have to win the war with the goblins today. That shouldn't be a problem, right?"

Radek glared at him. "What's going on with the Necal?"

"Oh right," Ovian said. "We were afraid they'd hear you, but I think we got lucky. They're breaking camp."

Radek stood up and looked toward the enemy gathering. They were starting to take down their tents, and the prisoners were standing in line. Fortunately, he and his friends didn't have anything to pack up, so they were ready to follow right away. Radek winced as he popped a ration tablet into his mouth. Ovian made a face but did the same thing. Brenna eyed one of the brown tablets and shook her head. Not for the first time, Radek envied the stamina that allowed dwarves to go for a longer period of time without eating. By the time the Necal were dragging their prisoners along, Radek and his friends were less than a hundred yards behind.

"You'd think they'd be more careful," Radek said.

"They're on the goblin homeworld surrounded by their allies," Brenna said. "They don't have to worry about anyone following. We should still be quiet though."

Radek nodded. The Necal moved even slower than the day before, stopping regularly. At noon, they roasted some kind of meat. The smell made Radek's stomach growl. They didn't feed the prisoners but seemed to take great joy in eating in front of them. After nearly an hour, they were off again. Before long, the dwarves led the prisoners into a clearing with half a dozen large buildings surrounded by an iron fence. The Necal passed through a gate that seemed to be the only way in or out, and Radek felt magical defenses spring up after they entered. The prisoners were brought to another group of dwarves. Something was said to them, though Radek couldn't hear any of it.

"What do we do now?" Radek asked.

"Wait for an earthquake, I guess," Ovian said.

"An earthquake?"

Ovian looked at the sky. "Venulia is an earth singer. If she didn't want us to rescue her, then she has to have a plan. That probably means an earthquake. Singer Dulan was also there, so I guess they could crush the buildings with plants or something."

"You know," Brenna said, "it is possible they're more subtle than you are."

Ovian snorted. "Once, she collapsed a canyon to destroy a goblin base. You don't send someone like her when you want subtle."

"There," Brenna said.

A lone figure approached the fence behind one of the buildings. Radek thought he heard a faint song. A few seconds later, the figure reached forward, and the fence parted as if it were made of cloth. Somehow, the song had also parted the defensive spells without breaking them. The figure nodded, turned back, and walked into the camp. Brenna smirked at Ovian.

"Not subtle, huh?"

Ovian glared but didn't say anything. Radek stood.

"She knew we were watching. I think she did this so we could get in."

"And do what?" Brenna asked.

"Free all the prisoners."

"Why can't she do it herself?"

Ovian looked to the sky. "There's only one way to find out."

Without waiting for the others to respond, he headed toward the camp.

CHAPTER 29

Radek reached forward and touched the iron bars. It felt like a curtain, and he could move them aside with ease. There were runes on the bars, but singer Venulia had somehow bound those spells to the bars so that they moved with the metal rather than being set off as Radek and his friends passed through. They crept into the prisoner camp. As soon as they stepped inside, words appeared on the wall of the nearby building, carved in Elven.

I know you are here. I will cause a distraction. Free the prisoners when I signal you.

"How do you think she's going to signal us?" Radek asked.

As if in response, the earth shook violently. Runes engraved on the nearby walls glowed brightly, and Radek recognized them as magic used to stabilize buildings. Their color shifted, and the magic contained within sputtered as the ground shook too violently for them to resist. Cries came from the other side of the camp, and Ovian smiled.

"See? I told you there would be an earthquake."

Brenna pulled out her blaster. "Do you really have to rub it in?"

Ovian thought for a second. "Yes, I really do."

Just then, an elf rounded the corner, looking terrified. Instantly, Brenna and Ovian went quiet. Radek waved the prisoner over. "This way. You can get out over here."

The elf ran toward them, tears streaking his face. He stopped in front of them. He was breathing heavily and babbled in Elven as he looked from one to the other. Ovian stiffened.

"No, we're not just children. Don't you know who we are?"

"It doesn't matter." Brenna moved the bars aside, and the elf's eyes went wide. "Go hide in the woods. Apparently, they hate the dwarves or something."

"They don't hate the dwarves," Ovian said. "They just don't like things driving through them."

"Do you think elves will be able to hide in them?"

Ovian looked at the sky. "Well, obviously."

"Then, what difference does it make?" She turned back to the elf and tried speaking in his language. "Go. Hide with logs. Wait for plant people."

The elf stared at her for a second but apparently got the gist of what she meant. He blabbered something in Elven before disappearing into the woods. Radek couldn't see him and had no idea if he was actually waiting for others, but Ovian seemed satisfied.

"Let's go."

The camp was in chaos. Prisoners had apparently broken free from whatever restraints held them. The Necal were trying to maintain order, but this camp had apparently not been built to withstand singers of Venulia or Dulan's caliber. Cracks had spread through the earth, swallowing Necal even as vines emerged from the ground, entangling the prison guards. The renegade dwarves, in turn, fired blasters at the singers, but there always seemed to be a vine catching the blast or a stone rising out of the ground just in time to block a shot. Most of Radek's time fighting in the war had been piloting *Wind*. While some magic could be used in that sort of combat, it generally wasn't the flashy kind. He hadn't ever seen a true elven battle singer in combat. If there had been a thousand Necal, it wouldn't have been enough. They could have been made of paper for how effective they were in fighting the singers. Then, the rune mages arrived.

Four of them came out of the main building with what looked like a layer of liquid steel covering their body like armor. Runes glowed brightly on its surface. A stone the size of Radek's head tore itself out of the earth and flew at the dwarves. It was still a few feet away when it shattered. Even so, that many rocks moving that fast should have torn the rune mage to ribbons. Instead, they bounced off of him like grass blown on the wind. The rune mage threw his hand forward. A wave of force so dense that it distorted the air shot at the earth singer. Her eyes went wide, and she sank into the ground like it had turned to water. A second later, she appeared behind the rune mages. They were apparently expecting it because two of them spun. They lifted their arms, and a net of green energy fell on her. Brenna raised her blaster and shot one of the mages, but a rune on his right side glowed purple. The blast hit the armor and spread over metal but didn't seem to have any other effect. Brenna grimaced and aimed directly for the rune but missed it by a few inches.

"I knew I should have been practicing this instead of flying around in a dragon fighter."

Ovian snorted. "Like you would have ever picked target practice instead."

He threw his hands forward, and a blast of wind shot at another of the mages. Once again, a rune on his armor deflected the spell. Ovian scowled.

"That really isn't fair."

Radek tried to summon power to himself and managed a tentative grip. "Maybe I can do something."

"No," a woman's voice said. "We need to get out of here."

Ovian went pale, and his hands fell. For a second, his mouth moved but no sound came out. Radek looked at the speaker. The elven woman had ragged clothes, and her arms and face showed signs of wounds, both old and new. It was her eyes that caught his attention. They were orange, a color that was so rare among elves that Radek had only known one who had them. Elven legend even said that an elf with eyes that color had dragon blood.

Ovian finally managed to speak, though his voice was as much a squeak as anything else.

"Mother."

CHAPTER 30

Radek stared at Ovian's mother. They had all believed Malen had died when *Vanel* had exploded. No one had even considered the possibility that she had been captured. Seeming to read his mind, she inclined her head.

"The first wave of goblins took prisoners to question us about elven defenses."

"You've been a prisoner for six months?" Ovian asked.

Rocks ripped out of the ground only to be broken by a dwarven rune before they could fly at their targets. Another singer shot a ball of fire that made the building it hit go up in flames. Radek coughed at the smoke in the air.

"Maybe we shouldn't talk about this in the middle of a Necal prison camp while they're having a battle," Brenna said.

"Your dwarven friend is right. We need to get off the planet. I have vital information that the fleet will want to have."

"What is it?" Ovian asked.

"Ovian, not now," Brenna said. "We don't exactly have a way to get off of Goalton."

"The Necal have a number of ships in a chamber beneath one of the buildings. There's a hatch outside the camp, but the entrance is here."

"Oh good," Ovian said. "I like this plan."

"Stealing a Necal ship?" Brenna asked.

Ovian nodded. "We always try that plan. It usually turns out okay."

"You mean with a ship that's disabled and about to be crushed in the atmosphere of a gas giant?" Brenna asked.

"Or a sun," Radek said. "One time, it was a sun."

"And we survived," Ovian said. "There's no reason we can't do it again. Besides, do any of you have a better idea?" He waved at his mother without waiting for them to answer. "Where are those ships?"

Vines had entangled several of the Necal. Singer Venulia had hurled a boulder at the front gates, tearing them open, and most of the prisoners were heading in that direction. Radek had to jump to one side to avoid a purple beam of light that one of the rune mages shot at him. Venulia opened the earth beneath that one. She didn't acknowledge Radek and his friends before continuing the battle.

"Come, while the rune mages are distracted."

"Shouldn't we take the others?"

"It would be too obvious. We can tell the fleet where they are. Now that most of the prisoners are out of the camp, the runes on this place won't hide them from elven scanners anymore."

"But—"

"We don't really have time to argue," she said as she headed toward the largest of the buildings.

Ovian followed after her without saying anything. Brenna grabbed Radek's arm before he took three steps.

"Don't you think it's a little odd that we happen to find Ovian's mother here? This can't be the only prison camp on the planet, so why is she here?"

"She's an important person. It makes sense that they would question her."

"But why would the goblins give her to the Necal instead of questioning her themselves?"

"Maybe they didn't realize who she was, or maybe it was the Necal that captured her in the first place, and they never told the goblins. Does it really matter? It's his mother."

Brenna hesitated for a few seconds before nodding, and they followed Ovian into the building. It was a prison. Jail cells lined the walls, and the rancid smell coming out of them told Radek that they had been where at least some of the prisoners had been housed. He stepped in something wet and tried not to think of what it could be.

"They hid their ship underneath the prisoner's living area?" Brenna asked.

"It's the biggest building," Mistress Melan said. "Anyway, I don't think the Necal built this place. They just got it from the goblins and used what was already here."

"No," Brenna said, "this is definitely dwarven built. There's even runestone built into the structure. No goblin could work with that."

Malen looked toward the ceiling. "Well, then, I don't know. I do know there are half a dozen Necal ships under this building. It's the best way off the planet."

"Lead the way," Ovian said.

Brenna grabbed Radek's shoulder and spoke softly. "Don't you think this is a little too easy?"

"Which part?" Radek asked. "The part where we were shot down, the part where we had to destroy our own ship, or the part where the goblins sent an army of ghosts to take down our fighters?"

Brenna glared at him. "The part where we just happen to encounter Ovian's mother who just happens to know where a ship is that we can steal to get off the planet."

"The Necal underestimated us," Malen said.

Both Radek and Brenna looked up at her. Brenna's face darkened a little as the elf tapped her ears. Ovian scowled at Brenna, and unshed tears welled in his eyes. He turned away and moved closer to his mother.

"Most of the prisoners knew there was something beneath this building. To be frank, no one, including myself, thought we would ever make it out of here alive, so the Necal weren't too concerned about what we saw. There's a secret hatch in one of the cells. Once, they forgot to lock it, and I was able to sneak a look."

"But if you could get in, why didn't you use the ship to escape?"

"Because I have no idea how to fly a dwarven vessel. I assume you do, and unless I'm wrong, we should get down there before any of the guards think to check in here for any prisoners too foolish to have escaped yet."

Brenna clenched her teeth but nodded. Ovian's mother led them to a cell in the back of the prison. It was surprisingly clean, even to the point of smelling better than other cells. Brenna raised an eyebrow at that but didn't say anything. Mistress Malen stamped on the ground with her foot several times until she found a spot that sounded hollow. She smiled, but Brenna's words gnawed at Radek.

"Brenna, can you scan the ground and see what's there?"

The dwarf nodded and pulled out her pocket computer. She tapped the screen a few times. "There's a big room. It looks empty, but I can't be sure. It's shielded, and I can't see any details."

"Which makes sense," Ovian said, "if there was, for example, a hidden docking bay with a secret Necal squadron."

Brenna tensed but didn't say anything. Malen observed the conversation with a mute smile. Once everyone looked to her, she scanned the area. "There's a rune on that wall that should open the way. Can you activate it?"

"How did you get in last time?" Brenna asked.

"They were careless. They left it open."

"If it's a sealing rune, it wouldn't have mattered. It would have closed on its own."

Malen let out a long breath. "Young lady, I know almost as little about dwarven magic as I do about dwarven ships. I have no idea why I was able to get in."

Ovian motioned her forward. "Just see if you can open it."

Radek could tell she wanted to argue, but she also wanted to get off the planet. She walked over to the wall Mistress Malen had indicated and ran her hand over it. She was much more inclined toward the technological than the magical, so Radek didn't know how likely it would be that she would be able to open a rune-based lock, but after a few seconds, she gasped and placed her hand on a stone. A brilliant green rune came to life under her hand.

"It's simple," she said. "It's a rune of opening, but there's no locks on it. It would react to any dwarf, but that doesn't make sense. They have dwarven prisoners here. Any of them could have gotten out this way."

"There aren't as many of them as there are of us. They kept them in a different building."

"But didn't you even talk to them? Any one of them could have opened this for you."

"This was a prison, not a social gathering. They watched us too closely."

"But not closely enough to notice when you snuck a peek at their secret hanger?"

"I told you. They got careless. Are you going to open it or not?"

"Do it, Brenna," Radek said, not entirely sure Brenna didn't have a point. "What other option do we have?"

"We could escape with the two powerful elven singers like the rest of the prisoners."

"Or we could tell the fleet where they are," Ovian said. "Venulia and Dulan both would probably agree if they knew about the ships."

Brenna pursed her lips and nodded. Her arm tensed and then twisted. There was the sound of stone grinding against stone as a piece of the floor moved aside, revealing a long staircase that descended into darkness. Mistress Malen started down right away. Ovian tried to follow, but Radek grabbed his arm. The elf glared at him, but Radek ignored him and turned to Brenna.

"What do you see down there?"

She squinted, but her dwarven vision failed her, and she shook her head. "Not much. It goes to a big room, but I can't see any ships or anything from here."

"Radek, this is my mother."

"That doesn't mean she can't be wrong. This feels like a trap. Maybe the Necal tricked her."

"If this is a trap, then that's even more of a reason for us to go down there. We can't just leave her to them."

Radek sighed, but Ovian was right. He motioned to Brenna, and they started down the stairs. As soon as they had gone a few feet down, the hatch sealed close again. In the same moment, dim lights came to life all along the wall. Almost instantly, Brenna tried to go back, but the hatch wouldn't open. She ran her hand around the perimeter but didn't find any runes. She turned back and glared at Malen, but the elf ignored her and continued down the stairs. Brenna stared for a few seconds before starting down after them. The whole situation made the hairs on the back of Radek's neck stand on end. He followed slowly, though Ovian was oblivious to his friends' hesitance. They reached the bottom of the stairs and looked around, but they saw no vessels, Necal or otherwise. It was just a big empty room, large enough to fit at least a half dozen fighters, but there was nothing in it. Malen, however, seemed not to be bothered and continued walking to the center of the room.

"We're trapped in here, now," Brenna said as she stepped off the stairs.

"Unfortunately for you," Mistress Malen said.

Pain shot up Radek's legs and filled his body. He tried to lift one of his legs, but it wouldn't respond. He couldn't even move. The cold power of goblin magic entwined with the hardness of the power given off by dwarven runes. The combined energy wrapped around him. He tried to grab onto it, but the pain restrained his mystical abilities every bit as much as it did his physical body. Ovian and Brenna had frozen as well. Only Mistress Malen was moving. She gave them a cold smile, and Radek thought his blood had turned to ice. Ovian's mother was a traitor.

CHAPTER 31

Radek tried with everything he had to move, to summon his power, to do *anything*, but the paralyzing magic held him firm. Mistress Malen laughed. The shadows cast by the dim lights gave her an evil look.

"Well, that was easier than we thought it would be."

"M…Mother," Ovian said, sounding like it took the effort of moving a mountain to get that word out.

"Oh, come now," she said, "You've known there was a traitor for a long time."

Radek could almost imagine Ovian wilting before those words. A year before, someone had been able to hijack *Wind* to take her to a Necal ring ship. Something like that would have only been possible if someone had detailed plans of the ship's programming. There had been other indications as well: goblin fleets where they shouldn't be, ambushes, and other traps that succeeded where they should have failed. It had to be someone high up in the elven hierarchy, someone like the wife of the elf in charge of *Vanel*, and a powerful singer in her own right.

"Don't worry," she said. "The paralyzing spell will wear off soon, but I wouldn't get my hopes up. This room is heavily warded, and even your human friend's penchant for destroying magical constructs won't get you out of here."

"Why?"

Radek had no idea how Ovian had managed to speak, but Malen just laughed. She walked behind him, and the sound of her footsteps on the stairs echoed in the room. After a few seconds, he heard the grinding sounds of the access hatch opening and closing. Then, they were left in silence. The paralyzing spell lasted a few minutes. Abruptly, the pain vanished, and Radek collapsed to the ground, gasping. Brenna got up first and went to help him up. His knees were shaky at first, and it was a few seconds before he could stand unaided. Then, they went toward Ovian. The elf wasn't moving. Radek's heart raced. Elves were closer to plants than animals, and Ovian's nature had led them into problems before, but it only took a moment to ensure that their friend was breathing. He opened his eyes and gave them a blank stare.

"Ovian, are you okay?"

"My mother."

Radek put a hand on his shoulder. "I know."

"She led us into a trap." He shook his head, and Radek could barely understand his sobs. "She can't be a traitor. She just can't be."

"Maybe they blackmailed her," Brenna said in a surprisingly gentle voice. "Goodness knows the goblins have almost killed us a bunch of times. Maybe she made a deal with them to keep you safe."

Ovian sat up but wilted after a second as he wiped away tears. "If that were true, she never would have led us into a trap."

"There could be some other explanation."

"Like what?"

Brenna pulled out her pocket computer and tapped the screen a few times. Then, she smiled. "I don't know, but I do think she left us a way out."

"What do you mean?"

"There's a cable that runs under the floor. If we can get to it, I might be able to access their systems. We might be able to open the hatch we came in through. If she was right about this being a secret hanger, then there could even be another way out."

"How are we supposed to get access to underground cables?"

Brenna raised an eyebrow. "You're an elven singer. Do some magic."

He glared at her, but Radek thought he saw the hint of a smile on the elf's face. He started to sing, and to Radek's surprise, he could feel the shape of the spell his friend was working. When he'd first heard the elven songs, they vanished from his mind the instant he heard them. Even as Radek had progressed to the point where he could manipulate elven magic, he had always done so by sensing spells with his mystical senses. He had never been able to tell what something was supposed to do just by hearing the song, but apparently, he had spent enough time with elves that that was no longer the case. Ovian's specialty had always been air magic, but he had limited talents in other areas as well. Like his mother, he knew something about the manipulation of plants.

The ground beneath their feet shook, and a panel on the ground rose up a few inches. Ovian was sweating as it was lifted higher by roots that looked too flimsy to pick up such a heavy piece of stone. They threw it aside, and it shattered with a sound that was probably heard throughout the prison camp. Beneath was a series of wires and cables. Brenna smiled as she knelt down next to the opening. She held her pocket computer over the wires and tapped the screen. Then, she reached down and grabbed a wire coated in red plastic. She retrieved a small knife from her pocket and cut the plastic away before laying her computer on top of it. The screen glowed even brighter, and there was the smell of ozone.

"I'm in. Give me a second to see what I can do."

Goblin letters appeared on her screen, along with an occasional image that resembled blueprints. Ovian looked over her shoulder, studying the screen intently, though as far as Radek knew, the elf understood neither goblin writing nor their schematics. Brenna looked back at him but didn't say anything. After a few minutes, the far wall slid open, and Brenna's grin widened.

"They really should put better security on their systems."

Suddenly, her pocket computer beeped, and her eyes went wide. She tapped the screen, but a bolt of blue energy shot up her hand. She yelped and dropped her computer. A crack spread across the screen, and they all stared at it. There was another beep and a hiss, this one at Brenna's pocket. She cried out and pulled the metal box that held all that was left of *Wind*. Dragon magic welled up inside of it, though Radek had no idea what it was doing.

"Brenna, what's going on?"

"They got into my pocket computer, and they're using it to access *Wind*'s personality module."

"Well, stop them!" Ovian said.

She picked up the computer. Again, the bolt of blue energy ran up her arm. Patches of skin blackened, and she gritted her teeth. She whimpered but managed to hold on. She tapped the screen so hard more cracks spread throughout it, but it wasn't responding. She threw it on the ground and stomped on it with her foot. The pocket computer shattered, but the module kept beeping, and the dragon magic flared. Brenna's face went dark.

"I have no idea how."

Ovian pulled a crystal from his pouch and sang, imbuing it with an amber glow. He grabbed Brenna's runestone necklace and pulled so hard that the string broke. Most of her runes went flying, but Ovian seized one of the squares out of the air and held it to the crystal. He then put them both down on the cable.

"Radek, blow it up!"

"What?"

"We have to save *Wind*! Use your power and blow it up!"

"I don't know…"

Both his friends gaped at him, and Radek stopped. Ovian was right. He had to do something, no matter how desperate. He reached into Ovian's crystal, a heat one of the kind they had used to survive in the coldness of space. Brenna's rune allowed her to breathe in low oxygen environments. The two magics weren't exactly compatible, but then, he didn't need to combine them. He just grabbed them and shoved them together, forcing them to join. Dwarven and elven magics were so different that they tended to violently oppose one another. This was no different. The crystal and the rune square fused together. They both took up a golden glow and shone so brightly that they hurt to look at. The magic coming out of them was a hundred times stronger than either of the spells alone. Radek grabbed it, and it burned him, body and spirit alike. He felt like it would rip him apart, but he didn't dare drop it. Without knowing exactly what he did, he forced the magic into the cable. Power ran through the entire room, and lines of light appeared on the walls and ceiling. Ovian doubled over as if in pain. Brenna ran over to him and said something, but Radek couldn't make out the words. The power was everywhere. It was too much.

Then, it all stopped.

Radek was on the ground, though he didn't remember falling. His skin tingled, and his elbow throbbed, apparently from him having landed on it. He had to try to stand three times before he actually managed it. Ovian was leaning on Brenna. Though her rune necklace had been magical, she had purchased all those runes. She had no magical talent to speak of, and consequently, the surge of power Radek had sent through the building hadn't overwhelmed her senses like it had for Radek and Ovian. Together, she and Ovian helped Radek to stand. He motioned to the metal box, which Brenna had dropped at some point. She looked at it and shook her head.

"I don't know. Without my pocket computer, I can't tell if you stopped it in time."

"He did, not that it will do much good," a deep voice said.

They looked up to where the wall had slid aside. The room opened into a large cave that wound into the darkness. The air just inside the cave shimmered. Then, as if coming from behind a curtain, a dragon stepped out of the air.

CHAPTER 32

The dragon was small, as such creatures go. Radek doubted it stood a dozen feet tall. Where most dragons he had seen could have swallowed him whole, this one would have to take at least four or five bites, not that that would do much good. Its scales were emerald green. Rania had said that a dragon's scales changed in response to their environment. Most dragons, having lived in stars for hundreds of years, had turned red long ago. If this one was green, that could only mean one thing.

"You don't live in a star," Ovian echoed Radek's thought.

The dragon looked itself up and down and then spread its wings. Even in the dim light, its scales glimmered like emeralds. It smirked at Ovian. "Obviously not. In answer to your question, your friend did indeed stop the transfer before the Necal got what they wanted."

"Which is what, exactly?" Brenna asked, her hand resting lightly on her blaster.

"Oh, don't be ridiculous," the dragon said. "Just because I don't live in a star doesn't mean I couldn't. A blast of energy from that pitiful thing isn't going to do anything. What the Necal wanted was a copy of your ship's personality file. It's the last thing they need to finally duplicate its technology. They thought to use a remote link in the dwarf's pocket computer to download it, but we never thought you'd actually bring the module itself with you. That will make things much simpler."

"What?" Radek asked.

"Oh, don't get me wrong. What you did was impressive. I don't think even the Shaper Derek had your talent for the raw destruction of magic. If the building hadn't been insulated to protect against exactly that, who knows how much damage you could have done?"

Radek clenched his teeth. "Derek. You work for the goblins, then?"

The dragon chuckled, wisps of flame coming out of its nostrils. "Little mortal children, my kind do not *work* for the goblins. They serve our purposes."

"Our?" Ovian asked. "How many of you are there?"

"You don't really expect—"

Brenna fired. The blast hit the dragon in the snout. It blinked as smoke streamed from its nostril. It cocked its head and looked like it was going to laugh. Brenna fired again, though this time, she missed entirely.

"I told you, you should practice with that thing," Ovian said.

"I haven't exactly had time."

The dragon drew back, and an orange glow came from its mouth. Ovian threw his hands forward and sang. Fire erupted from the dragon's mouth at the same instant that wind surged forward from Ovian. It was much smaller and more concentrated than the air blasts he usually used. It rushed into the dragon fire. For a moment, the flames seemed to hover in the center of the room. Then, they turned back before dissipating. Ovian squealed with joy.

"Yes! It worked."

"You came up with a spell to deflect dragon fire?"

He nodded. "I've been working on it ever since we fought that dragon on the ring ship."

"That was a year ago." Radek was impressed. Ovian had always been impulsive and almost childlike. It was easy to forget that he was also a powerful singer. If this war had happened a hundred years in the future, he might well have been one of the hundred singers called to enchant the Hope Diamond.

The dragon roared and spread its wings. Had it been larger, it wouldn't have been able to lift off in this room, but it rose into the air. No sooner had it done so, though, than another blast of wind brought it to the ground. It tried to rise, but the wind held it down. Brenna gaped at Ovian.

"You're fighting a dragon."

Ovian was sweating, and he spoke through clenched teeth. "Shoot it."

Brenna nodded and fired, hitting the dragon half a dozen times. Most of the shots bounced off its scales, but one tore through the wing, and another went into its mouth. The damage was insignificant, though, and the dragon got to its feet and rushed forward. Ovian tried another blast of wind, but his spell apparently lacked the power to stop a dragon charging on the ground. It snapped at Radek, who fell back, barely avoiding its teeth. Ovian cried out as the dragon's tail slammed into his stomach. It didn't bother going after Radek. Instead, it focused on what it thought was the greater threat: Ovian. As it moved forward, it didn't pay attention to Radek. Or to Brenna.

The dwarf lifted her blaster and fired. This time, she didn't miss. The blast hit the dragon in its right eye, turning it into a circle of blackened flesh. It reared up and roared so loud Radek thought his ears would bleed. The dragon had said that the room had been insulated against Radek's abilities. That meant magic had been used to craft it, and if that was true, then maybe Radek could use it.

He opened himself and reached into the ground with his mystical senses. He thought he felt something and tried to grab onto it, but it was like trying to grab onto smoke, and it slipped through his fingers. He tried again. It was more solid, but it was like holding onto water instead.

"I can't do anything with it."

Brenna and Ovian had split up so that at least one of them was on the dragon's blinded side. Each time it tried to take off, Ovian held it down, and the elf was able to deflect its fire blasts even when it attacked Brenna. Neither one of them acknowledged Radek's words. He felt useless, but if his friends could fight off the dragon without him, then that gave him a chance to try something else.

The creature rushed at Ovian, and Brenna peppered it with a dozen shots. Ovian dove to one side and tossed a crystal in Radek's direction. He caught it, sensing the - within. Once again, he tried to reach into the magic of the room, but he had no more success than last time. In desperation, he reached for the dragon. It actually took a second to laugh as it looked at him.

"Do you think we don't know about you? I'm not about to use my magic, not when I can so easily kill you and your friends without it."

Brenna ran up behind the dragon, but it didn't notice. She reached into her belt pouch and pulled out a small square engraved with a dwarven rune. She slipped it into a compartment in her blaster and aimed. She held down the trigger. Nothing happened for a few seconds, but she kept the weapon raised. The dragon started turning toward her, and her eyes went wide. She shook her head at Radek, and mouthed something, but he couldn't tell what. Regardless, he knew that if the dragon saw her, she was dead, so he spouted the first thing that popped into his mind.

"If it's so easy, why haven't you done it already?"

The dragon focused on him, smoke streaming out of its nostrils. It ran right at him, but just before it hit, Brenna's blaster went off. The red energy beam seemed to burn itself into his vision. It hit the dragon's head with the force of a starship at full speed. It drove the dragon into Radek. He screamed as its weight came down on him, but a second later, a blast of wind pushed him free. The dragon shuddered as it struggled to rise. Burned and blackened spots marred the back of its head. Brenna, meanwhile, was on the ground, gripping one hand in another. Her blaster had melted, and there was still smoke rising from the hand that held it. Radek ran to her to see if she was okay.

"I got that rune to use in an emergency." She smiled, though it seemed forced. "I guess it worked."

The dragon looked from them to Ovian and back again. It eyed the blaster and gave a smile that sent a chill down Radek's spine. It rushed at the elf. He tried to leap aside again. Though the dragon had been slowed significantly by its injury, it was still more than fast enough. It seized Ovian in its mouth. He screamed and tried to sing, but the dragon squeezed tighter. Radek and Brenna both rushed forward, though he had no idea what they could do. The dragon gave a muted roar, and Radek could just make out the orange glow coming from behind his friend.

"No!"

The fire consumed Ovian before it rushed at Radek and Brenna. Radek lifted his arms and tried to call on his power. He felt something and seized it as the heat brought tears to his eyes. He thought he heard Brenna scream, but it was impossible to be sure over the roar of the flames. He actually felt his spirit leaving his body as the fire burned him to a cinder amidst a flood of dragon magic.

CHAPTER 33

Radek woke up, which was a surprise. He'd had close calls before. Once, he'd been in a ship that had been torn apart by the gravity well of a star just before he and Ovian had fallen in. That time, however, he had lost consciousness. He hadn't actually *felt* himself die like he had now.

He wasn't sure where he was. There was just a gray haze as far as he could see. He called out, but his voice had a hollow quality to it, and it barely even sounded like words. He extended his mystical senses and shivered. This wasn't cold like goblin bone magic was cold. This was the cold of the grave. This was death magic, only it was constant, and it was everywhere.

He concentrated power into his voice. That caused the haze to swirl around him. It surprised him so much that he almost lost control, but he managed to focus his magic into a single word.

"Hello?"

His voice was strange. It seemed like it should have echoed, but it just sounded flat. The haze quivered, but otherwise, there was no response. He took a step forward. His feet made no sound on the ground. In fact, he couldn't even feel his own weight as he walked.

He bent down to touch the ground and found…nothing. He wasn't standing on anything. His hand went below where his feet were, and he could even bring it up to touch the bottom of his shoe.

"Well, this is odd," he said, and once again, his voice had that strange incomprehensible quality to it. This time, however, something responded.

It was a hollow call that filled him with a primal terror. He would have run, but he knew deep down inside that he would never be able to get away. This thing was like the wind. It was more than that and somehow less at the same time. There was no escaping something like this.

He shook his head and tried to clear away the thought. He recognized the impulse as mental magic. The fear wasn't real, but as the thing howled again, he wasn't so sure. Radek tried to call power to himself. Where most of the time, that had been an uncertain proposition at best, this time, magic rushed toward him, filling him to a degree he hadn't known was possible. For a second, he just held the power, stunned. The thing called out again, but this time, the cry just slid off of him, and as it did, he understood a part of it. He knew exactly where it was.

He ran through the featureless gloom without tiring. His legs didn't ache. He didn't even breathe heavily. The power in him was too strong. It wasn't long, though he couldn't be sure if it was seconds or minutes, before he found the creature.

It was Ovian.

The elf looked at Radek with tears streaming down his eyes. He was transparent and seemed spread out as if he were made of air. He opened his mouth to try to speak, and Radek heard the same call that had scared him earlier. The sound carried all of Ovian's terror. He clung to Radek's hand, but Ovian wasn't solid enough to hold on, and their hands passed through each other. Not knowing what else to do, he focused his power on his friend. Something solidified, and when Ovian tried to speak again, words came out.

"Radek, what happened to us?"

"I'm not sure," he said, though he was beginning to have a suspicion.

"Have you seen Brenna?"

"No."

However, as soon as the word left his lips, he felt her presence through the haze just like he had felt Ovian. He took his friend's hands and ran in another direction. Something dragged at him, and he turned to realize that Ovian wasn't actually running. Radek was dragging him along with no effort whatsoever.

"Radek, what's going on?"

"Brenna's right over here."

The ground shook, the first time since waking up that Radek had felt it do anything at all. He found Brenna just standing in the mist. She started to look toward them, but her movements were glacially slow. Ovian was closely aligned to the element of wind, but Brenna was of the earth. As before, he surrounded her with his power. It infused her, and she took a deep breath. She looked around, and her eyes went wide.

"Are we dead?"

Ovian's jaw dropped, and as he looked around, he went pale. More pale. Now that Radek knew what to look for, his friends seemed to have drained of color. He looked down at himself and saw the same was true of him. Even the mist seemed muted.

"I think so."

"Where…" Ovian took a deep breath. "Where exactly are we?"

Radek looked around. "The underworld? I guess."

"I don't think the underworld looks like this," Ovian said. "Can't you just bring us back to life?"

Radek stared at him. "Bring us back to life?"

"Yeah, you studied death magic, right?"

"I had one lesson, and that definitely didn't cover using magic as a ghost to bring myself back to life. In fact, I'm pretty sure Stregoi said it was impossible."

Ovian let out a breath and threw up his hands as if Radek was being completely unreasonable. Radek rolled his eyes and concentrated.

"Let me see what I can do."

Again, he felt that coldness, but he tried to reach past it. There was something solid there. He pushed and somehow knew that he lacked the power to go beyond it. He moved along it, feeling for any weaknesses. The flaw was so slight that he almost missed it, more like a place a flake had been chipped away than a crack. He focused on it. He thought he could go through it if he tried. There was something on the other side, but whether it was back to life or further into death, he had no idea. One thing he was sure of. There would be no coming back if he did that. He only considered for a second before extending his hands.

"Hold on."

Dimly, he was aware of his friends taking hold of him. Then, he concentrated his power and forced it into the weakness. He screamed and heard Brenna and Ovian doing the same, but he allowed his power to carry them forward. The next thing he knew, the world of the living rushed toward them.

CHAPTER 34

They found themselves back in the chamber they had died in. The dragon was nowhere to be seen, and the wall had closed. The lights had gone out, but somehow, he could see even better than he had when they were on.

"You did it!" Ovian said.

"That was way too easy," Radek said.

Brenna walked over to the wall that hid the cave entrance and placed a hand on it. She passed right through it. She looked back at Radek and shook her head.

"Ghosts," Radek said. "I had no idea I could do that."

"I don't think you're supposed to," Ovian said. "I didn't think ghosts could bring themselves back without help."

"Then why did you ask me to bring us back?"

Ovian looked at the ceiling. "Well, we were dead. It's not like anything worse was going to happen."

"He does have a point," Brenna said.

Radek glared at her. "Since when do you agree with him?"

She shrugged and looked at the ceiling. "There are necromancers aboard the *Linala*. Maybe one of them could help us. It's not like we need a ship to fly anymore. Or to breathe in space for that matter."

Ovian nodded, and for a moment, Radek reflected on the fact that he and his friends had lived a life so strange that they took even dying and coming back as ghosts in stride. Finally, he shrugged. "Does anyone have any idea how to fly?"

"You were doing it earlier."

"I was?"

"Yeah, when you were taking me to Brenna."

"I was just running."

Ovian lifted an eyebrow. "On what?"

Radek opened his mouth to answer but stopped. There hadn't been anything to run on. The ground, or whatever it was, hadn't actually existed. He hadn't been thinking of flying, though. He just knew where he needed to go. He had sensed it. He closed his eyes and reached out. He was a ghost. In a way, he *was* death magic. He could feel its reflection in himself. Necromancers, especially those as powerful as Stregoi, would almost have to have an effect on this ghostly realm. His senses couldn't reach all the way into space, but at the edges of his senses, he could detect a faint warping. He tried to run there, and when he opened his eyes, he was in the air, heading for the ceiling. His legs kicked uselessly in the air. He stopped moving them, but still, he continued his ascent.

"How are you doing that?" Brenna asked.

Radek started to explain, but he couldn't find the words. Rather, he just scooped them up, somehow doing so even though they should have been out of reach. Together, they floated up, passing through the ceiling as if it weren't there. The prison camp was empty, and Radek wondered how long they had been in that foggy void.

They passed the highest building, and the sky lit up in a brilliant green flash. Pain filled him, and the next thing he knew, they were falling, far faster than gravity could account for. He screamed as the ground rushed up to meet them, but they passed through it without feeling a thing. The room they had been trapped in passed in a blur as they went deeper. Even in the dark of solid matter, they could see each other. Both of his friends were terrified, though Brenna seemed to be calming. Before Radek had a chance to speak, they passed into empty space and stopped.

Bones of all different sizes had been haphazardly jammed together to form the walls and floor of the room they found themselves in. Some of them had been plated with gold to allow them to access dragon gold magic, while others had been arranged in the shape of dwarven runes. Some were so huge that they could have only come from dragons or similar sized creatures. Radek didn't see anything that could be a way out. There were other ghosts there, too, so many that the horde sent after the attacking fleet seemed tiny by comparison. Some of the ghosts noticed the newcomers, but most continued to wail in horror. The sound was like needles being driven into his skin. Radek moved his friends closer to him and used his power to hold off the worst of the screams.

"What happened?" Brenna asked.

"I think the goblins set a trap," Radek said.

Brenna cocked her head. "A trap in case the goblin's dragon killed us, and we came back as ghosts, and then we tried to fly to the *Linala*?"

Radek pursed his lips and nodded. "You have a point. This probably wasn't meant for us. It's probably how they captured the rest of the ghosts, though." He indicated the horde around them. "This has to be a whole planet's worth of ghosts."

"More than that," Ovian said as he pointed.

Most of the ghosts here were goblins, but a fair number were humans, elves, dwarves, and a scattering of spirits of other races of the Vanelian Compact.

"Why are they here?" Brenna asked.

"So the goblins can control them," Radek said.

"No, I mean, they sent a horde after the fighters, and that was more than they could handle. If they were to send this many spirits against the fleet in orbit, they wouldn't stand a chance, so why haven't they done it?"

"There aren't controlled," Radek realized, "at least not completely. Look at them. These spirits are being tortured."

"Is that what's going to happen to us?" Ovian asked.

"Not if I can help it," Radek said.

He called his power to himself. It wasn't the rush of energy he had felt in the haze, but he managed to take hold of it.

"Ovian, give me a crystal."

Ovian patted his pockets. "I don't actually have anything."

"Well, just start singing!"

Ovian hesitated before opening his mouth. The sound that came out, however, was nothing like elf song. It was a wail that, had Radek been still alive, would have driven all happiness and joy from him. Some of the other elves had joined in the song. Radek reached out but sensed no elf magic in their music. Rather it was a form of death magic that could practically tear through flesh, provided it had enough power to actually touch that world. He tried to mix it with the bone cage that held them, but it was no use. The spell the goblins had crafted had been built specifically to defend against death magic, which was all these ghosts were. Without mixing magics in some form or another, Radek couldn't break through. As strong as the walls were, he wasn't sure he could do it even if that had been true elf song.

"I think you're all banshees."

Ovian stopped singing, but the rest of the spirits cried out even louder, and Radek could feel the anguish in them. He tried to speak to Ovian and Brenna, but the sheer volume of the cries drowned out his voice. Even his power seemed useless, like he was trying to stop a tidal wave with his hands. He managed to draw Ovian and Brenna closer to him and shield them from the worst of it, but he knew he wouldn't be able to resist it for long. He didn't know how long it was before the cries finally went silent.

"Does that mean you can't do anything?" Ovian asked.

"I'm not sure yet. Your singing is all death magic. My power is too, so I can't combine them to make anything blow up." He ran his hands along the bone cage. It felt solid, which was an odd sensation in his ghostly form. "I might be able to do something with this."

"You are a shaper," an elven ghost said as it approached.

Radek inclined his head even as he summoned his power to himself. The spirit seemed not to notice and drifted closer. It stopped a few feet in front of him.

"One of your kind built this cage."

"My kind? A human, you mean? Before I died, anyway."

"No, not your kind as you were. Your kind as you are now."

"Dead?"

The ghost nodded, and Radek went absolutely still. A dead shaper. One who was allied with the goblins. He knew of such a shaper. He had hoped that the death of that shaper had been his end, but now, it seemed like that wasn't the case. He almost didn't want to say the name. Ovian said it first.

"Derek. You mean Derek is here?"

"Indeed," a familiar voice said from beneath them.

The ghosts scattered. Radek resisted the urge to back up as a spirit rose up out of the bones forming the ground. He was tall, and even in death, he had a bald head. The eyes were as cold as the void of space itself, and he radiated power that was very nearly cold enough to freeze the spirits around them. Derek looked at the three of them and smiled.

"Well now, isn't this a surprise?"

CHAPTER 35

Radek didn't wait for Derek to say anything else. He had already gathered his power when the elf had approached earlier. He flung that power at the dead shaper, intending to destroy it if he could. Derek crossed his forearms before him to catch the blast. The force of the attack still drove him back, but an instant later, he waved his hand, driving Radek's power around him.

"You've improved," he said. "Now why don't you…"

Brenna, who had snuck around the shaper, slammed her fists into the back of his head. If they had been living, it would have, a least, knocked him out. Apparently, things weren't that simple among spirits. Derek flinched. Then, without turning around, he threw his hand back, hitting Brenna with a blow that was more magical than anything else. She flew through the air and slammed into the far wall. A wave of green energy washed over the bones, and Brenna slumped to the ground.

"You still haven't learned to be polite…"

Ovian threw his hands forward and sang. Rather than a rush of wind, however, what looked like a congealed shadow shot forward, writhing as it moved. Derek brought up a hand to meet it, and though he stopped most of it, a few drops splashed onto his face.

"Oh, come now. Do you really think a banshee's wail…"

Again, Radek threw his power at the shaper. This time, some of his attack got through, and Derek staggered. He waved a hand, and a bone arm shuddered under Radek's feet before reaching up and grabbing his hands. It forced him to the ground. He could move his head just enough to see that Ovian and Brenna had been similarly restrained.

"The three of you are incredibly annoying," Derek said. He smiled. "You're getting stronger, Radek, and you've adapted to this new form quickly. I'm impressed."

Radek tried to glare, but he couldn't raise his head enough to meet the ghost's eyes. "I don't really care that you're impressed. What are you doing here?"

"The same thing as always, helping the goblins. When I sensed a spirit as powerful as you enter my trap, I just had to see who it was. I didn't expect you."

"I won't join you, so don't bother asking."

"Join me?" Derek laughed. "The time for that is long past. No, I think I'll just focus my efforts on breaking you until you serve the goblins as faithfully as any other. They were quite annoyed with you when you prevented them from accessing your vessel's personality files."

"What happened to her?" Ovian asked.

Derek shrugged. "The memory module was destroyed when your bodies were incinerated."

"Dead?" Ovian asked.

Brenna didn't wait for a response. "Why are you doing this?"

The shaper smirked. "Why do I want to get revenge on the boy who killed me? What a mystery."

"Killed him."

The phrase echoed through the imprisoned spirits, and Radek felt the grip on his hands weaken. One of the elves began to sing in that terrifying voice. Others soon joined in. Derek screamed, and Radek realized that what he heard before from the banshees was a general cry. It hadn't been directed at him like it was now aimed at Derek. The bones holding Radek down crumpled. He got to his feet just as Derek waved a hand and created a dome of energy around himself. The same darkness that Ovian had thrown at Derek now surrounded him, but the banshees' cries were eating away at it. The same elf that had approached Radek before came near.

"You truly killed him?"

"Not exactly," Radek said. "I mean, I destroyed his mind. I wasn't really sure if he survived that."

"But it was you that banished him from the land of the living."

"Yes, I guess so."

"Can you defeat him again? Send him from this place?"

Radek looked to the dome of blackness. He could feel power gathering within, and he knew that the ghostly assault could not hold Derek for long. He let out a breath. "I have no idea."

"But there is a chance." The faintest glimmer of hope reflected in the spirit's face. He pointed to where the arm had come from. "Aim your power there. The shaper used part of his own spell to entrap you. He had to weaken it in order to do that."

"That makes sense," Ovian said, causing Radek to jump. He looked up to see both of his friends at his side.

"When did you get here?"

"Right when the other banshees trapped Derek," Brenna said. "Are you going to get us out of here or what?"

Radek laughed and extended his senses to the ground. Just like the dead elf had said, there was a weakness there, but he felt more than that. A flood of information entered his mind. It was all numbers and calculations. If he focused, he thought he could even see the molecular makeup of the bones. He didn't understand how that could be, and he put that out of his mind for a second. Radek forced his power into the weakness. He pushed it apart, but he could only open it by an inch. He looked back at the black dome trapping Derek. It pulsed, and there was an occasional flash of blue from within. He didn't have much time. He returned his attention to the weakness and tried to push it further apart.

"What are you doing?" the banshee aside. "You're not physical beings anymore. That is more than wide enough."

Radek blinked at him, and after a second, he nodded. Once he thought about it, he thought he knew how it was done. He allowed himself to slip into the hole and was dimly aware of pulling his friends behind him. He felt it closing even as he passed through it. A second later, they were in a wide cavern. Above them, a cube that seemed to be made of thousands of bones hovered in the air. It emanated a cold power, and now that he was outside of it, he could sense the mixture of dwarven, goblin, and dragon magic. He reached out for it, but it was like touching a wall, each brick made from a different material and held seamlessly together. He found the spot he had escaped from, and there was a weakness there. He was relatively sure he could break through, and maybe even shatter the spell entirely. Of course, that would only free Derek, and they needed time to get away.

"We should go."

Brenna looked around. "Do you have any idea how to get out of here?"

Ovian glanced upward. "I think we just fly through the ceiling."

"That didn't exactly work out last time."

"So we don't fly into the sky. We just fly until we're at the ground. Then, we find whatever is trapping ghosts, and Radek figures out a way to get past it."

Radek blinked. "I do?"

Ovian made an exaggerated eye roll. "You always break that stuff. Even that dragon said you were good at it."

"I might not be able to do it while I'm dead."

"You won't know until you try."

Radek sighed. "I guess you do have a point there."

They flew through the ceiling and into solid rock. Radek thought he could almost feel his essence sliding through the stone. It made his skin crawl. He kept his senses open. The cube keeping the ghosts prisoners burned like cold fire in his mind, but it wasn't what pulled them in. They had been going for a few minutes before he thought he sensed what they were looking for. He called out to his friends and pointed. They nodded, and he headed off in that direction.

The power grew stronger as they approached, and Radek could almost feel it pulling at him. Before long, they passed into a cave. Radek squealed as something tried to pull him forward. There was a skull on a pedestal, glowing with the power of goblin magic. More than that, however, it was a dragon bone.

"That's it," Radek said. "It's what's trapping the ghosts."

"Can you break it?"

"I'll try," Radek said, reaching out.

"Oh, come now," a deep voice said. "You don't really expect me to allow you to do that, not after allowing the goblins to use my own skull, do you?"

Radek blinked. He had been so focused on the spell that he hadn't thought to look for anything else. Power pooled just beneath the surface of the ground. It rose up, and Radek took several steps back, almost without realizing he was doing it. This dragon was at least three times bigger than the one they had already fought. Its head was covered in spikes, and ridged bones protruded from its scales. It was also a ghost, and it stared at them with an evil grin.

Brenna let out a long breath. "That is really not fair."

CHAPTER 36

White fire erupted from the dragon's mouth. Unlike the smaller one, this one didn't need time to get its breath weapon ready, and the fire washed over Ovian. Radek screamed, but even that was drowned out by Ovian's cry. The fire vanished, and Ovian was still there, without a mark on him. He had fallen to the ground and was breathing heavily.

"That hurt."

"You're alive," Radek said.

Ovian sighed and looked himself up and down before shaking his head. "No, I'm still dead."

The dragon laughed. "You haven't been dead for very long, have you? Ghosts can be destroyed, but nothing as simple as the fire of a dead dragon will do it." It grinned, showing its teeth. "That was just to cause pain."

It breathed fire again, this time at Radek. He threw up his hands and tried to summon whatever power he could to turn it aside, but the fire raged on, engulfing him. For a moment, all he knew was pain. There was death magic all around him, but he couldn't think enough to do anything about it. He screamed until he would have gone hoarse if he'd actually had a physical body. Then, the fire faded, and slowly he regained his senses.

"Why are you doing this?" Brenna screamed. "They killed you, didn't they? You said that's your skull. Don't you want revenge?"

"Revenge? Do you have any idea what it takes to turn a dragon into a ghost? Dozens of bone mages worked themselves nearly to death to manage it, and because of that, I will exist forever. Why would I want revenge for that?"

It breathed fire at Brenna. Radek reached for the death magic in the flames, trying to pull it away, but it refused to be moved and rolled over Brenna. She screamed even louder than they had. Radek pulled at the dragon's skull, trying to access the goblin magic powering it. When that failed, he tried to mix his own magic into it, but his power swirled around the skull before streaming into it through the eyes and mouth. Then, the skull pulled at *him*. Radek screamed, and with an effort, he shut away his power.

He turned to the dragon, and an idea began to form. His friends were in trouble, and so he didn't allow himself time to consider if it was a good one or a bad one. He just threw himself at the creature. It didn't even budge when he hit it, but Radek reached for the power within it, trying to draw it into himself. The dragon flinched. Radek knew he hadn't done more than a pinprick, but hurting it hadn't been his intention. His attack had gotten the creature's attention. He flew up and punched it in the nose. It looked more surprised than anything else. Then, Radek flew toward the skull. The dragon roared and breathed fire at him. He dodged it, and once again, tried to influence it. He could only move it a little, but it was enough. The fire hit the skull and was sucked in just like Radek's own power had been. A part of him was hoping that it would somehow break the spell, but it didn't work. The dragon cocked its head.

"Ah yes, I see. Your plan was to have my own power destroy it. Failing that, you wanted to enrage me enough to come after you.

Once I did, you would nudge me toward the skull and let its power deal with me. It's not a bad plan, if you were fighting an idiot. No, I think I'll just keep burning your friends."

White fire rushed toward Ovian and Brenna, but a shrill note pierced the air, and the fire stopped as if it had hit a solid wall. At first, Radek thought Ovian had done it, but the surprised look on his friend's face said he was wrong.

"You will not harm them, beast," a familiar voice said.

The expression on Ovian's face went from fear to shock to disbelief and finally to joy. The elf that stepped through the wall stood tall with an aura of authority that only came from a lifetime of leadership. Somehow, he smiled at Radek and his friends even as he scowled at the dragon, and for the second time that day, Ovian stared at a parent he thought he would never see again.

"Father."

CHAPTER 37

Veelan Javin inclined his head before lifting a hand to the dragon. Even the skull seemed to grow brighter in response to the elf's presence, and for the first time in a while, Radek thought they would be okay.

"Let them go," Javin said. "I will not permit more harm to come to them."

The dragon snarled. "You can't stop me, banshee."

"Yes, I am a banshee, and when I made that transformation, I gained power that I never had in life. You, on the other hand, are only a shadow of what you once were. Who do you imagine is greater now?"

Smoke streamed out of its nostrils. "I will gain back what I have lost."

Javin gave a half-smile. "Perhaps in time. In a century or two, you might begin to reach the same level of power you had, but that is still a long way off, and it won't help you today." He took a step forward. "You will let them go."

"I think not."

Javin's face went hard. He screamed. Like had happened when Ovian and the other banshees screamed, what looked like congealed darkness shot forward, but this was somehow deeper, more consuming than any Radek had ever seen before. This was very nearly death itself given form. It slammed into the dragon and hissed. The dragon threw back its head and roared. There was power in its voice but not nearly as much as the Veelan's. Javin screamed again. This time, the blackness splashed against its right side and crept over fully half the dragon's body. It tried to roar once more, but it had apparently sustained too much damage. Its essence seemed to be draining away. It gave a cry that was closer to a whimper than a roar before backing away and disappearing into the wall. Veelan Javin turned back to them.

"Hello, son. I admit I didn't expect to see you on this side, at least not anytime soon. What happened?"

Ovian looked at the dragon skull. "One of those things killed me. It burned me up, so I don't even know if there was anything left."

"There wasn't," Brenna said. "At least there wasn't when we got back."

Both Ovian and Radek nodded. Javin put a hand on his son's shoulder.

"Believe me, son, I understand. I doubt there was anything left of me either."

Ovian drew back. "I'm sorry. I didn't mean to."

"No, there is no need to apologize."

Ovian looked at the ground. "I killed you."

"You issued a command. Nothing more. If you hadn't, do you imagine that the goblins would have let me live? Or anyone else on that station, for that matter? No, son, put away this guilt of yours."

"That's easy to say," Ovian said.

Javin bowed his head in concession. "True enough."

"Can you help us break that thing?" Radek asked.

"Unfortunately, no. It is difficult to affect the physical world as we are, and the spell on that skull was designed specifically to absorb death magic. Anything I can do would be sucked in just like the dragon's fire was."

"How about helping us get off the planet?" Ovian asked.

The ghost shook his head. "Again, I'm afraid not. This spell traps anyone who flies too high."

"Then, what do we do?" Ovian asked.

Javin looked to the skull, and it pulsed with a hungry light. He shuddered and took a step back. "We get out of the dragon's lair, for one. That beast will be informing its masters soon, and I'd rather be far away when it returns."

"Father, the traitor."

Javin raised a hand. "Not now. We can talk about all that later. We don't have a lot of time."

He waved for them to follow and disappeared into the ceiling. Ovian went after him without another word, but Brenna looked at Radek.

"Not this again."

"Brenna, you've met his father."

"I met his mother too. She was working for the goblins the whole time."

Radek bit his lower lip. "Well, we can't just let Ovian chase him by himself, and it's not like things can get any worse."

"Unless he leads us into another trap."

"He ordered Ovian to blow up the station to preserve our secrets. That doesn't sound like something a traitor would do."

Brenna paused for a second before nodding. "You have a point there." She looked toward the ceiling. "We'd better go before we lose them."

It was surprisingly easy to follow the two elves. Though there were dozens of feet of solid wall between them, Radek sensed exactly where they were, and he pulled Brenna along after them. After a few minutes, they stopped, though they were still in the middle of solid rock.

"Why are we stopping here?" Ovian asked. "Shouldn't we find a cave or something?"

"You're still thinking too much like the living. We have no need for empty spaces." Indeed, all Radek could see was darkness around them, but the other ghosts were perfectly visible to him. "Now, what were you saying about the traitor?"

Ovian took a deep breath and looked away. "It was Mother."

Javin cocked his head. "What was Mother?"

Ovian looked to Radek and Brenna before answering. "Mother was the traitor. She's the one who sold *Wind*'s plans to the Necal, and she--"

"No." Javin's voice was as hard as steel.

Ovian blinked. "What?"

"No, you're wrong. It wasn't your mother."

"Father..."

"I've known her for centuries and loved her most of that time. She is no traitor."

Ovian looked away. "She led us into a trap that got us killed. She admitted it to me just before she left us to die."

Javin's face hardened. "I said no, son."

"But..."

"Wait, are you saying she's on the planet? She wasn't killed when *Vanel* was destroyed?"

Ovian was obviously holding back tears. "No. We found her in a prison camp."

"If she was a prisoner, then she was no traitor." He spoke like it was the most obvious thing in the world. "Take me to where you saw her. Maybe I can make contact with her."

"Father, you can't."

He waved off Ovian's words. "You haven't been a ghost for very long. She can see more than most. If we're both there, my bond with her will be enough for her to see us."

"Father, she…"

"Is your mother and my wife. If you're not going to help me find her, I have my own ways. Now, take me to her, or I'll find her myself."

Ovian looked like he was going to cry. Finally, he turned to Radek.

"I'm not sure how to find the Necal prison camp. Can you do it?"

Radek looked from Ovian to his father. After a few seconds, he nodded. He closed his eyes and reached out. He wasn't quite sure what he was looking for, but he realized he could sense something, a familiarity that both felt like home and terrified him if he looked too closely. When he opened his eyes, both Brenna and Ovian were pointing in that direction. Ovian looked a little embarrassed.

"I can feel it too. I think it's the place we died."

Veelan Javin turned around and looked upward. He nodded once and spoke softly. "We can all feel where we died."

Radek shivered as he realized he had been looking at *Vanel*. "How did you get here? We're fifty light-years from the station."

Javin met his eyes. "This is where I can serve my people best. Where else would I be?"

Ovian was a flighty elf, and at times, he acted like a boy half Radek's age. Other times, though, he had put everything aside for the sake of his duty. For the first time, Radek realized how much of that had come from his father, an elf whose sense of duty had taken him across the stars. He nodded. "It's this way."

The peculiar sense which located the place of their death didn't have any way to determine distance, but somehow, he thought he knew exactly how far it was, to the foot. He told himself he was imagining it. Once they had a location in mind, they moved quickly. Traveling through the earth was an odd sensation. He felt like he shouldn't be able to see, but yet he never lost sight of his friends. He could always sense them as well with his mystical senses. More than that, if he focused, he could sense anything alive around him, from the roots that had wormed their way into the earth to the insects that burrowed through the rock. It only took them an hour to cover the distance. As they progressed, his mental estimation of how far they were steadily shrunk. He detected the roots Ovian had made grow in the room long before he reached the underground chamber.

"Here," Radek said. "She led us into a trap here, but she left before the dragon showed up."

"Yes, I can feel her."

"You can?"

Javin blinked. "Spirits such as us are held together by our connections. I can sense that she was here, and I believe I can follow her." He looked the three of them over. "I know what you think, but I'm telling you, Malen is no traitor. I'm going after her. You are welcome to come with me, but I understand if you don't wish to."

"We're going with you," Ovian said. He turned to his friends, pleading in his eyes. "Right?"

"Yes," Brenna said, "of course we are."

Radek looked at her, and she glared back, but no one said anything. Ovian's father, oblivious to what went on between them, flew up to the top of the room.

"Be careful," he said as they neared. "The entrapment spell will catch you if you go too high. We need to stay close to the ground."

He didn't wait for them to respond before he took off into the forest. It was an eerie sensation, flying through almost the same path they had walked through before they had died. It wasn't long before Radek realized where they were going.

"The chamber where they had the eggs."

"I should be surprised by that," Brenna said. "Somehow, I'm not, though. Is she here? Have you detected any elf magic?"

Radek shook his head as they reached the opening Rania had left in the ground. Veelan Javin stopped and stared down at it before turning to the three of them. He inclined his head in respect.

"This was one of the most heavily defended places on the planet. I assume the three of you had a hand in this?"

"Rania did," Ovian said.

"Your dragon friend is here? Good. She did her work well. It looks like the defenses are down."

He drifted down into the hole, but even Ovian hesitated this time. "The crystal banks on Droshala are guarded even against spirits, and those spells are independent of the physical aspects. Even if someone knocked a hole in the wall, I don't think the magic would go down."

"So, you think this is a trap?"

He looked after his father descending into the hole and bit his lower lip. "I don't think my father is leading us into a trap, but then I didn't think my mother was either."

"He might just be blinded to the possibility." Brenna let it hang, and Ovian slumped his shoulders.

"Or maybe I know her better than any of you suspect," Javin said.

Radek jumped and saw that he had come within a few feet of them without then noticing. They had been talking softly enough that their words should have gone unnoticed even by elven ears.

"You heard us?"

He smiled. "You have a lot to learn about being a ghost. How good the ears were in your physical body has absolutely nothing to do with how well you can hear now. It's a matter of will and concentration. You can move faster than we have been too, if you're of a mind. At least you can if you're not following a trail. I'm not walking into this blindly. I'm keeping my senses aware in case of a trap, and as I've just shown you, they are rather more developed than yours."

Brenna shuffled on her feet, and Javin looked toward her. "But that doesn't take into account the possibility of me leading you into a trap, does it?" He turned toward the pit that had once held the dragon eggs. The cold power of goblin bone magic practically radiated from it. "Especially if I'm leading you into that."

Radek bit his lower lip but stood up straight. "Well, yeah."

"I don't know what I can say to convince you. As I said, stay behind if you wish. I don't imagine I will be away long."

"She did lead us into a trap, father."

"And there are a dozen possible reasons I can think of for her to do that, not the least of which is that she's been tortured into submission."

Panic danced across Ovian's face. "Do you think so?"

"It's a possibility. I won't know until I see her."

Ovian nodded. "I'll go with you."

He looked to his friends, and Brenna shrugged. "We're not going to leave you alone now."

Radek nodded as well, and the three of them followed Ovian's father into the goblin pit. Radek just hoped they weren't heading into a trap.

CHAPTER 38

Radek sensed magic as they went down, but it was far away, nowhere near what it should have been, especially with what he had felt a little while ago. In a way, the lack was almost more eerie than all the bones. There was power here, though somehow it had been hidden from his senses. He could touch the walls, and he could only fly a short distance before he had to walk. The others were having similar problems.

"This is starting to look more and more like a trap," Radek said.

"Indeed," said Javin. "Be careful."

In spite of that, he walked faster. Radek and his friends had to maintain a jog to keep up. It wasn't long before they came into the chamber covered on all sides with bones. The ceiling was still intact, so the Vanelian attack had apparently failed. A group of goblins and dwarves were speaking in one corner of the cavern. Radek tried to listen like Veelan Javin had described, but he couldn't hear more than a faint mumble, even as they got near. There was a robed figure, and at first, Radek thought Derek had somehow managed to come back to life, but as they grew close, he saw the pointed ears of an elf. Both Ovian and his father froze as the light revealed the face inside the hood. Radek found himself looking at the orange eyes of Mistress Malen.

Ovian put a hand on his father's shoulder. "I'm sorry."

"No, there is more here than meets the eye."

He waved a hand, and there was a shattering sound. The voices suddenly sounded clear.

"We still have no idea how they were able to transport so many ships here so quickly," a dwarf said, "but it doesn't look like they're able to do it again, or we would have been overwhelmed by now. We should launch an attack."

"They have surprised us before," Malen said.

"I think your host is getting to you," a goblin said.

"Host?" Ovian asked. "Does that mean…"

"I knew there was something else going on," Javin said. "She's been possessed. Maybe all of them have been."

"Can we do anything to help her?"

"Yes. Do you know how to manifest physically yet?"

"No," Ovian said. "We haven't really had time."

"Then, be ready to stop anyone who shows up on this side."

"What do you mean?"

Without bothering to respond, a surge of death magic swirled around the elf. As one, the gathered people looked to Veelan Javin. He opened his mouth and screamed. The same blackness rushed forward, but this was different, less solid. It hit the closest dwarf, and for a moment, Radek thought he saw stone cracking as the blackness wrapped around him. Then, the dwarf just collapsed. Javin targeted a goblin next. That one raised a hand with a bone bracelet. It glowed with cold power, but after a second, it exploded in a shower of sparks, and the goblin too collapsed. Once again, Javin attacked. By this time, though, the goblins had joined together. Three of them managed to hold off the power of the scream. One of the dwarves held up a rune, which glowed a fiery red.

Ovian went to stand beside his father. He too screamed. The darkness that came from him didn't have the same spectral quality to it, but it slammed into the goblin shield and hissed. The shield bent inward as Javin continued to scream. A crack spread across its surface. The dwarf's eyes went wide, but before he could do anything, the shield split in half. Both Ovian's and his father's attack rushed forward. Ovian's passed right through the goblins, but Javin's wrapped around them. For a second, they seemed to be resisting, but it only lasted a few seconds before they all went to the ground. The dwarf stared at Javin in horror before turning and running away, leaving only Malen.

"Will you scream at me, too, my love?"

"Fight it, Malen. Fight it."

"Fight it?" she laughed. "Do you think she hasn't been trying to fight me for the past year?"

"Well, that's all I needed to know," Ovian said.

He screamed. Again, the darkness passed through his target, but this time, she flinched. Ovian's scream apparently lacked the ability to affect the physical world, but if his mother really was possessed, then it was the spirit that he needed to reach, and if it was truly spirit, then it could be affected by death magic.

Radek called power around himself. He could feel…something inside of Mistress Malen, but it was like a shadow or a reflection. He focused his attention on her more deeply, and his perception of her sharpened. The spirit possessing her had slipped around Mistress Malen, like an oily residue on the surface of the water. He tried to grab it, but it slipped through his fingers. He tried again, but he had no greater success than the first time. More than that, he sensed Malen writhing in pain as he tried. He didn't see how to do this, at least not alone.

"Ovian, scream again."

For once, the elf didn't question. He just opened his mouth and screamed. This time, Radek didn't see the blackness hit Ovian's mother. He did, however, see the effect. The oil quivered and separated from the water slightly. Radek shoved his power between them, forcing them even farther apart. There was a scream, though Radek wasn't sure if it was the ghost or the woman it inhabited.

"Keep screaming," he said with clenched teeth.

A second scream joined Ovian's, and the oily substance almost seemed to slip off of Mistress Malen. It tried to hold on, but Radek lashed out with his power like a whip, and the last tendrils of the spirit's link to the body came free.

Radek fell to his knees, exhausted. His vision blurred, and he lost his balance when he tried to get up. "I think she's free."

"Radek," Ovian said. Radek blinked several times to clear his vision while Ovian kept speaking. "We didn't think this all the way through."

"So what else is new?" Brenna asked. "Can you two hold him off while Radek recovers?"

"Hold who off?" Radek asked as his vision came into focus.

Picking himself off the ground by Mistress Malen was the ghost of the biggest goblin Radek had ever seen. It stood up, towering over all four of them. The energy radiating off of it could have frozen the sea. It stalked toward them.

"Javin, Ovian?" Malen spoke with tears streaming down her cheek. "Was that you?"

"A little busy, Mother," Ovian said, though Radek wasn't sure she could hear him.

Ovian screamed, and that same darkness shot forward. It wrapped around the giant ghost. It didn't seem to notice as the darkness wrapped itself around his chest. It kept going forward. Ovian's father screamed as well, but his attack had no more effect than his son's. The ghost continued to approach and swung his ethereal club at Javin. The elf sank into the ground. Ovian moved behind the goblin and started singing. More of the blackness slammed into the goblin's back.

Radek lashed out with his power. Even Brenna tried to do a few things with her pistol. Radek had no idea how she had kept it through dying, but then again, he somehow had clothes on, so maybe it was the same thing. Still, her blasts passed right through it without making the goblin so much as flinch. Ovian's father rose out of the ground less than a foot away from the creature. He screamed right in his face, focusing more power than Radek had ever felt from a banshee. Cracks spread through the stone ground, and rock dust floated from above. The goblin ghost staggered back but then lunged at the elf. Its fingers extended into claws, and its face elongated, growing sharp teeth that were as long as Radek's fingers. Javin bent as if he was made of rubber. The goblin growled. It seemed to liquify as it hit the ground. It dashed under Javin and shot at his back in the form of a spear. It stabbed into him, coming out of his chest. Javin grimaced, but then, he turned around, passing through the goblin spear as if it were…well, a ghost. He screamed, and the darkness that shot from him shattered the spear. Radek thought he had won, but the pieces melted and then flowed together, reforming into the goblin. It wore a wicked smile, and its voice was like metal grinding against metal.

"It's been a long time since I met a spirit who could move as you do. Impressive."

Ovian's father screamed again. This time, the goblin expanded, catching the blackness and hurling it back at the elf. Javin dodged, but a few drops of it splashed on him. He was getting tired, or whatever passed for tiredness in ghost. He seemed thin and more wispy than usual. The goblin, on the other hand, didn't even seem winded.

"He's drawing power from the bones," Ovian said.

Radek walked over to a bone and tried to kick it. His foot slammed into it. Pain shot up his leg, but it didn't budge. He knelt by it and pushed, but nothing happened.

"They're too well-grounded against the dead," Radek said. "Someone living has to do that."

All three of them turned to look at Mistress Malen. Then, Ovian and Brenna looked to Radek.

"Can you do it?" Brenna asked.

"I'm not sure. I saw Javin, but…"

He closed his eyes and called death around him. It swirled, catching him up in it. He could feel the barrier with the world of the living, but it stood firm. He threw his power against it, but it had no effect. Finally, he let it go. His head was pounding and aching more than he thought a dead person should be able to hurt. Javin and the goblin were still engaged in combat, though their shapes shifted so quickly that Radek couldn't tell one from another.

"I can't break through."

"Javin said being a ghost was all about connections," Brenna said. "You don't exactly have one with Ovian's mother. It has to be Ovian."

"But I don't know how to manifest," Ovian said.

"Maybe I can help with that," Radek said.

He called death again, but this time, he directed it at Ovian, surrounding his friend. Once again, he felt the barrier, but this time, it bent with barely an effort. Ovian reached out, and the barrier flowed around him. All of a sudden, he was on the other side. Malen gasped.

"Ovian? You're…" Tears welled in her eyes. "Oh no. I did this, didn't I? I killed you."

"A dragon killed us, but that's not important right now."

"How can it not be important?"

"Because Father is fighting a super-powered ghost who is drawing power from all the bones, and we need someone living to wreck the constructs."

She blinked, but when she opened her eyes, the tears were gone, and she had a look of resolution on her face. Her eyes seemed to glow with an inner fire, and Radek realized it wasn't just from his father that Ovian got his dedication. "Tell me what to do."

"Just wreck everything you can."

She nodded once and started singing. On *Vanel*, Mistress Malen had primarily been responsible for taking care of the tree homes of the elves. Ovian might be skilled at the manipulation of plants, but she was a master.

Her voice echoed throughout the cavern. Roots and vines shot out. Some grabbed bones while others broke straight through them. Radek sensed the goblin power trying to resist, but it hadn't been designed to stand against a physical assault on such a wide scale. There was too much magic for it to simply dissipate, but bolts of energy shot from one end of the cavern to another, completely at random.

"Mother…"

"Don't worry about me," Malen said. "I've been in more dangerous situations than this."

What looked like a cage of vines came out of the ground and surrounded her just as a bolt shot at her. It hit one of the vines, which shriveled as it prevented the energy blast from hitting her.

"I need to get out of here," she said. "Find me when you can."

Using the vines like tentacles, she practically flew out of the cavern. The goblin ghost roared as Javin pulled himself away from it. The goblin was panting. It stood up straight and took a step. As soon as its foot hit the ground, Javin screamed again. The darkness slammed into the other ghost who cried out in fear just before it dissolved. Javin smiled before falling to his knees. His form wavered, becoming transparent for a second before solidifying.

"Father," Ovian said, flying to his side.

"I'm sorry…to leave you again."

"What?"

"That fight took too much out of me. Radek, come here. Ovian doesn't have the skill in death magic to accept this."

Radek did as he was told. Javin stood on shaky legs and stared into his eyes. Death magic swirled around him. He opened his mouth and screamed. This time, however, light shot forth instead of darkness. It surrounded Radek. He could feel it pressing against his mind. It wouldn't be able to break through, not unless he allowed it. Veelan Javin was fading more and more by the second.

"Please."

If he delayed more than a few seconds, Javin would be gone. He didn't have time to think about it. He called death magic to himself and drew the light in. His mind exploded with knowledge. Everything Javin had known about being a ghost filled him. The next thing he knew, he was on the ground, and Javin was gone.

CHAPTER 39

Radek?" Ovian cried. "What happened? Where is he?"

Radek brought a hand to his forehead and shook his head. "I'm sorry. He's gone. We should go find your mother."

Ovian nodded without saying a word, and the three of them floated toward the cave Malen had gone through. Her passing had apparently disrupted the power of the bones, allowing them to fly and giving them access to their other ghostly abilities.

They found Mistress Malen at the same entrance they had gone in when Rania had first brought them here. She was manipulating the plants on the mountainside. Radek landed next to her, Ovian and Brenna did the same. Radek called death around himself. This time, however, he had Javin's knowledge. He hadn't even imagined there was so much to know. The wall resisted, but he didn't have to go through it. He bent around it, taking his friends with him. Malen gasped as they appeared.

"Javin?"

Ovian shook his head but didn't say anything. Finally, Radek spoke. "He sacrificed himself to save all of us."

For a second, Radek thought tears would form, but she clenched her teeth and waved to the plants. "I grew those in the form of an elven code. Rescue should be coming soon."

"Won't the goblins recognize it?" Brenna asked.

Ovian shook his head. "We were working with plants even before our people left Earth. Most other races would see natural growth, but the elves will know."

"They lost a squadron attacking the boneyard."

Malen nodded and brought a hand to her forehead. "The ghosts. They have to attack the control chamber."

"Twenty-seven degrees north. Ninety-five degrees west. A quarter-mile down," Radek said.

Ovian blinked. "How do you know that?"

Radek paused. "I don't really understand how. I know the coordinates of where we are, and I know exactly how far we've come from that chamber. It's like something is feeding me the information."

Ovian hesitated for a second. "If we tell the fleet that, they can target it from space. It's a lot smaller than the boneyard."

A shadow passed over them, and it startled Radek so much that he lost his grip on his magic. Malen retreated into the cave, but a few seconds later, Radek recognized the form of Rania. She circled a few times before landing. She looked right at Radek, even though he wasn't manifested. Her expression wilted.

"Oh, Radek, I am so sorry. I never should have left you alone."

If he had still been alive, a lump would have formed in his throat. "We were hoping that with death magic..."

Rania was already shaking her head. "There were stories long ago of the dead being brought back, but that magic was lost long before the races left earth. No magic I know of can break through the barrier from this world to the next to bring a soul back."

Radek and his friends exchanged glances. Ovian and Brenna seemed to fade a little, and he would not have been surprised to learn that he was doing the same thing. He nodded once and tried to keep his voice steady.

"We know how the fleet can get past the ghosts."

He proceeded to tell her the coordinates. Rania inclined her head and spoke after a few seconds. "I have communicated it to the rest of the fleet."

It took him a few seconds before he could speak. "We destroyed *Wind*."

"I know. When I created her, I never imagined she would play such a pivotal role in the fate of the galaxy. She gave her life for this cause, the same as you."

"What do we do now?"

"Ghosts remain because they still feel like something is holding them here. Once the war is won, I believe you will dissipate."

Ovian brightened a little. "You mean we're going to win?"

Above, a squadron of starfighters flew toward the control chamber. They moved slower than they were capable of, and Radek realized they were escorting half a dozen merfolk bombers, which had the strongest weapons of any vessel save the dragon ships. The ground shook as Rania spoke.

"With the boneyard destroyed and the ghosts no longer protecting the planet, the goblins can no longer stand against us. There's only one thing left."

A shadow fell over them. Radek looked up to see a blood-red dragon standing on the ridge above them with its wings spread.

"Grr'ink'itor," Rania said.

"You fought me off in the space around your allies' station, but now, you are on the world of *my* subjects, a world orbiting *my* star, and I have a feeling your friends will be much less able to resist once you are gone."

Fire shot out of his mouth. Rania tried to get out of the way, but she wasn't fast enough. The fire crashed into her, and she roared, blasting the goblin dragon with her own flame. He managed to avoid it as he took to the air. Rania roared again and flew after him. She was the faster of the two, and her teeth latched onto his leg. He flailed and slashed with his claws.

A streak of white shot out of the ground. Radek had just enough time to recognize Derek before he disappeared into Rania. The goblin dragon let go of her, and she writhed in the air, somehow staying aloft in spite of the fact that her wings weren't flapping. Radek watched in horror as Derek's magic spread throughout her body. In a second, it was over, and the possessed dragon spread her wings and roared in triumph.

"What do we do now?" Ovian asked.

Radek's eyes wandered from Rania to the goblin dragon. He had seen Derek do it, and Javin had also known how it was done. At least he did for humanoid beings. He had no idea if it would be the same with dragons, but he didn't see any other options. He rose off the ground and shot at Grr'ink'itor. He sank into its body and pitted his will against the dragon of the goblin star.

CHAPTER 40

Radek felt like he was being strangled. The dragon was all around him. He could hold it off from one direction, but that didn't help when it came from everywhere at once. It was huge, with a power that was almost too much to be believed. He summoned death around himself. That weakened the dragon's assault, but not by much. It squeezed him, and he knew it would destroy him in a few seconds.

"Radek?"

With that word, the pressure on him lessened. It spoke from a shapeless void, and it took Radek a second to be able to think enough to recognize the voice.

"Brenna?"

"I'm here too."

"Ovian? What are you two doing here?"

"What, you're the only one that can jump into a dragon?" Ovian's voice asked.

"Um, I guess not. Even your father didn't know more than one ghost could possess something."

Though he couldn't see his friend, he had the impression that Ovian was looking up. "Neither did I, but it seems to be working. I guess. I can't control anything, though."

Radek turned his attention inward. The three of them were holding off the dragon, but as he tried to spread out, he got tangled in the souls of the others. They were doing the same.

"I think only one of us can be in control," he said.

Both of the others withdrew at once, holding the dragon's will back rather than trying to control it. He sensed more than he heard their intentions.

"Radek, you do it."

He spread himself out through the dragon's body. It tried to come at him, but Brenna or Ovian stood in its way. While they couldn't stop it entirely, they did weaken it enough for him to fight it off himself. Then, all at once, he could see.

Radek had always suspected dragons had better senses than humans, but he'd had no idea how superior they were. He could see the leaves rustle as wargs ran through the trees. He could smell the great worms burrowing through the earth, and through some other sense, he was aware of the ghosts trapped in the bone cage, though it was miles away. If he focused, he could feel other dragons on the planet, though most were small, like the one that had killed them. One dragon shone to his senses. Rania.

The flapping of his wings didn't so much propel him through the air as it worked magic to carry him forward. Rania was ahead of him, but he knew he was stronger. He had access to more magic than she, especially when on a planet orbiting *his* star.

He flew through the air as fast as *Wind* had ever flown. Rania was there, ahead of him. She was flying toward the fleet. Radek flew faster. As far as anyone up there knew, Rania was an ally. If they didn't defend against her, Derek could decimate the fleet before anyone could do anything about it.

Radek opened his mouth and launched a ball of flame. It crashed into Rania, and she fell a few feet before recovering. It was enough, though. Radek seized her in his claws. She turned her neck and bit his right wing. The pain shocked Radek even as Derek's power lashed out at him. He let go, but before he had a chance to do anything else, Rania was half a mile up. Magic swirled around him, and his wings froze. He could practically hear Derek laughing. Radek gripped the magic and tore it apart. Then, he darted out of the atmosphere.

Pain exploded through his body as the fleet opened fire. Energy blasts tore through his wings, and missiles exploded against his chest, though fortunately, none of the dragon ships had been close enough. He turned and dove back down, out of range of the ships, struggling to stay aloft.

"We're going to try again," Radek said.

"Good idea," Ovian said. "It's not like we care if this dragon dies."

"That's not what I mean," Radek said. "Be ready to leave."

"What?"

Radek didn't take the time to respond. He shot up again. As soon as he left the atmosphere, he shot a ball of fire. It didn't hit any of the fleet, but it got close. Just like Radek hoped, they opened fire again. Radek left the dragon just before the fleet's fire tore into it, and he headed right for Rania.

This time, there was resistance. Derek held him back, but Brenna and Ovian joined him. Derek's defenses held for a second, but then they broke, and the three of them sank into the body. Once again, he found himself in a void.

"Last time, you were lucky," Derek said. "Today, I end you."

"Last time, Radek was alone," Ovian said.

"Now, there are three of us."

Radek seized his power and that of Ovian and Brenna. He felt Derek opposing them. Pain lanced through him, and he could feel the same in Ovian and Brenna, but suddenly, the knowledge of how to defend against Derek entered his mind. He interwove his power with that of his friends and made it as powerful as a ship's shield. Awareness flowed through Rania, and she too lent her strength. Derek's power bounced against his defenses, but Radek didn't let it end there. He threw it back at the dead shaper.

A missile exploded as it hit Grr'ink'itor, and having taken more damage than even a dragon of his power could stand, his life was finally snuffed out. His magic was another matter, though. Derek called to it as it passed from the world of the living, and it flowed into him. Once again, the shaper attacked, and Radek's defenses shattered.

"Three can be destroyed just as easily as one."

He ripped Radek and his friends apart, erecting a barrier between them and Rania that prevented her from helping.

"You need more help."

Radek recognized the voice. It was the same force that had given him such surprising bursts of knowledge. It was familiar, though he couldn't quite place it.

"Hello?"

"The ghosts. You know where they are."

"They're so far."

"No, they're not. Remember what Ovian's father said. Distance doesn't mean the same thing to us."

It did something, shielding him from Derek, though only slightly. It was enough, though. The voice was right. He could feel the trapped ghosts. He could feel the weakness he had caused when they escaped. He threw his will at it, and the prison shattered.

"Help me."

And then, they were there. A thousand ghosts rushed into Rania. Derek tried to hold them at bay, but as soon as he did, his focus on Radek lessened. Radek threw power at him, and he screamed. His defenses fell, and the ghosts ripped into him. Tearing him to pieces. Radek had seen how Derek had called Grr'ink'itor's power, and as that power left Derek, Radek did the same. The power was almost beyond imagining. The planet, the star itself, gave him strength. The voice came back.

"Like this."

Molecules, atoms, protons, and things even smaller. He knew them. He understood them. It would take a lot of power to do what he needed, but he had power to spare. Rania had said that no one could reach from the world of the living to the dead, but the power wasn't in the world of the living. Neither was he. He grabbed his friends and poured out his power, doing what no one thought was possible. The last thing he remembered was reaching for an egg.

CHAPTER 41

R adek woke up, and light hurt his eyes. An elven healer stood over him holding a crystal. Her eyes when wide, and she tapped a communicator on her wrist. Radek looked around. Ovian and Brenna were there as was Rania in her human form. All were in sickbeds. His body ached, and it took him a second to realize that was a good thing.

"What happened?"

"You won the war." Rania said.

"I did? How?"

Stregoi glided in on silent feet. He gave Radek a smile that sent chills down his spine. "I would be interested to learn that myself. I sensed a surge of death magic like nothing I've ever seen. The next thing we knew, the three of you were here."

"Radek brought us back," Ovian said.

"I did?"

He looked upward. "When something strange happens with magic, I think we can be pretty sure you're responsible."

"I don't think that's how it works," Radek said.

"He's right," Rania said.

"He is?"

"You used my magic, and that of the dead shaper Derek combined with what remained of Grr'ink'itor to reach from the world of the dead to the world of the living."

"You said that was impossible."

"I said I didn't know how to reach from this world to the next, but you apparently figured out how to do the opposite. You reached into this one. You manipulated molecules to form new bodies for yourselves, and then you deposited your souls inside."

"How did I know how to do that…The voice."

"What voice?"

"The whole time we were dead, I knew things I had no way of knowing. I thought it was instinct or something, but at the end, it spoke to me, and I realized it was real. It showed me exactly what to do."

"Another ghost?" Rania asked.

"A ghost who knew about molecular manipulation enough to recreate our bodies?" Brenna asked. "That's really specific knowledge. Who would know how to do that?"

"*Wind!*" Ovian said.

The three of them looked at Ovian.

"Ovian, *Wind* was a machine."

"But she was intelligent."

"An intelligent machine."

"Verren said he hadn't been able to duplicate the artificial intelligence in our ships. There was something special about her."

"Yes," Rania said, "her programming was born of dragon magic."

"Did you give *Wind* a soul?" Ovian asked.

Rania opened her mouth and then closed it again. She pursed her lips. "I don't think so, but Radek may have."

Radek blinked. "What?"

Rania inclined her head. "I told you, I detected a change after you intermingled your magic with hers. I think that may have been what I was detecting."

"It makes sense, Lady Rania," Stregoi said. "Objects, especially magical ones, can sometimes develop a personality of their own, especially if they are cared for and treated like a living thing."

"We certainly did that," Brenna said, sounding more and more unsure with every word. "Could we have given her a soul?"

"All of that together may have done it," Rania said. "It would have been a young one, probably not strong enough to have a form, even on the other side, but I suppose it is possible. Amazing, but possible."

"I…" Radek shook his head. "I don't even know what to say to that."

"Perhaps you can contact it," Rania said. "I would be interested in speaking to such a soul."

Suddenly Radek understood, and he couldn't stop himself from smiling. "You can't, at least not yet."

"What do you mean?"

"Where did you put the dragon eggs?"

"I hid them in my own star. I'll find another place for them as soon as I have time."

"*Wind* is in one."

"What?"

"I didn't realize what I was doing at the time, but I put her in one. How long will they take to hatch?"

"Five years or so."

Radek smiled. "Then, in five years, *Wind* will be born."

ABOUT THE AUTHOR

Gama Ray Martinez lives near Salt Lake City, Utah. He moved there solely because he likes mountains. He collects weapons in case he ever needs to supply a medieval battalion, and he greatly resents when work or other real life things get in the way of writing. He secretly hopes to one day slay a dragon in single combat and doesn't believe in letting pesky things like reality get in the way of his dreams. Find him at http://gamarayburst.com/ as well as http://www.facebook.com/gamarayburst

www.ingramcontent.com/pod-product-compliance
Lightning Source LLC
Chambersburg PA
CBHW020809190726
48285CB00006B/2219